J. H. Carey

The Marannos

A Tale of the Inquisition, during the Reign of Ferdinand and Isabella

(Spain's most Eventful Era.)

J. H. Carey

The Marannos
A Tale of the Inquisition, during the Reign of Ferdinand and Isabella (Spain's most Eventful Era.)

ISBN/EAN: 9783337030452

Printed in Europe, USA, Canada, Australia, Japan

Cover: Foto ©Andreas Hilbeck / pixelio.de

More available books at **www.hansebooks.com**

THE

MARANNOS.

A TALE OF THE

INQUISITION,

DURING THE REIGN OF

FERDINAND AND ISABELLA:

(SPAIN'S MOST EVENTFUL ERA.)

TRANSLATED FROM THE SPANISH.

San Francisco:

M. Weiss, Publisher and Printer, 319 Battery Street, cor. Commercial

1875.

PUBLISHER'S PREFATORY.

THIS, the first of a series of publications which the undersigned intends to issue at intervals, is herewith presented to the public. It is an historical novel, founded on events which occurred during the reign of Ferdinand and Isabella, of Spain—a reign which might be aptly named "the golden era" of that kingdom ; for it was then that the several States into which the country had been broken up for ages, were united and brought under one rule ; the kingdom of Naples was conquered ; the ancient empire of the Spanish Moors overthrown ; the dread tribunal of the modern inquisition established ; the Jews, who contributed so sensibly to the wealth and civilization of the country were—we will charitably suppose, only through mistaken bigotted zeal, and perhaps jealousy—not only banished but otherwise unmercifully persecuted ; and in fine, such changes were introduced into the interior administration of the monarchy as have left a permanent impression on the character and condition of the nation, but which also, dating from that period, entered upon its downward course. And in this place be it permitted to call attention to the curious fact, that from whichever country the Jewish nation has been banished, there shortly after commenced not only the downfall, we may say, of that country's power, but also the deterioration of its people. This is not said in the spirit of flattery, but history, in every instance, records it. Prescott, Helps, and other great historians, it is true, have given us a clear insight into the historical events of that period, but it is just the facts, brought to light again by these eminent men, that offer abundant material to the modern novelist to enlarge upon. Such is "THE MARANNOS," a novel translated from the Spanish—attractive and interesting— for which we ask the favorable consideration of the reader.

M. WEISS.

M. WEISS,
Book and Job Printer,
No. 319 BATTERY STREET,
San Francisco, Cal.

THE MARANNOS!

A TALE OF THE

— INQUISITION —

DURING THE REIGN OF

FERDINAND AND ISABELLA:

(SPAIN'S MOST EVENTFUL ERA.)

CHAPTER I.

THE sun had sunk behind the mountains of Antiquera; the valleys were wrapped in shade, and only the highest peaks still glittered in the declining light. A gentle freshness began to mitigate the sultry heat, and nature seemed to seek repose. But man was still untired; for around the walls of Granada lay the camp of the Spaniards, whose narrowing circles encompassed the besieged town like a brazen chain. Across the Xenil, floating bridges had been constructed, and these were filled with troops and cannon. The camp extended as far as Santa Fe, which was an entirely new town, and owed its existence to the protracted stay of the besieging army. Bright fires shone on all sides, and around them lay the wearied soldiers, resting from their fatigue, and passing the time in cheerful conversation, while ever and anon might be heard the tinkle of the mandolin, mingled with the rich voice of some captain, as he chanted the sweet words of a romance. A still greater activity prevailed at Santa Fe; for on this day had the crowned heads of Arragon and Castile, Ferdinand and Isabella, accompanied by a retinue of priests and nobles, made their entrance amid the shouts of their armies. Yet, although the freedom of the

neighboring camps softened somewhat the rigor of Spanish
etiquette, all gaiety was banished from the Court; for the war
with the Saracens had now lasted nine years, the flower of the
Spanish youth had perished, and the clergy (although the
cause was a sacred one), began to be sparing and reluctant in
procuring supplies. It was not, therefore, to be wondered at
that the forehead of the King was more furrowed than in his
younger days; only Isabella kept her usual serenity, upheld by
the certainty of success, and the consciousness of purity of
intention. Strangely contrasted with this bustle was the death-
like stillness which reigned in the besieged town. Companies
of Moorish soldiers gathered upon the walls, and looked down
upon the Spanish camp with rage and fury, for on that day
had the brightness of the Saracens' Crescent been dimmed by
the Christian Cross. Besides this, their minds were excited
by the pressure of want and the scarcity of provisions. The
streets were noiseless; the bazaars empty; only here and there
was seen the figure of a physician, whose Jewish extraction the
black silk caftan betrayed, conducted by torch-light to the
gates of some palace where a wounded nobleman waited his
aid. In the royal palace, however, some signs of activity
prevailed, although even this was more like consternation. The
chieftains of the army had just been dismissed by Mohamet
Boabdelin, whose heart was yet torn with grief for his early
friend Almanzor, whom he lamented far more than the thousands he had lost in that day's battle. When he returned
from his sally what a sight presented itself to him! The magnificent town of Granada resembled more a desert than a city,
the palaces were ruins; the noble buildings were ashes; and in
the public places lay jewels and treasure, worthless and untouched. The citizens, ghastly and in rags, crowded round
him to ask for bread; weeping women and moaning children
surrounded the soldiers and threatened to sap all their remain-
ing courage with their lamentations. Sad were the thoughts
of the twentieth ruler of Granada, as he looked upon the deso-
lated town, the sad remnant of glory maintained through nine
centuries, and angry were his words as he turned to the Grand
Vizier and charged him with the loss of one of the principal
ramparts. Repose refused to visit him as he sought it on his

gilded divan; for his heart was agitated by thoughts of revenge against his enemies for the loss of his friend and throne.

Suddenly Alharez rushed into cabinet, crying out: "Pardon ruler of the faithful, but I have important news! The Christian King and his consort have arrived in the camp."

"Whence did you gain this intelligence?"

"A Jew, whom our outposts intercepted as he was coming from Guadix, has brought the information. And his words are confirmed by the bustle in Santa Fe which we perceive from the walls."

"Where is the Vizier?" asked the King quickly.

"In the ante-chamber, bewailing the disgrace into which he has fallen."

"Let him come in without delay.—Vizier," said the King as Abdallah entered, "we must sally out this very night."

Abdallah stood amazed.

"Vizier, a sally," repeated the King, louder than before.

"My royal master," at length answered the Vizier composedly, "my life belongs to you and the faith of the Prophet, but your life is the only consolation left to your trembling subjects. Do not, then, let a sally add another defeat to our former ones. Our soldiers are terrified and wearied with the unsuccessful exertions of the day, while the Spaniards are intoxicated with victory and animated by the presence of their king."

"Am I not a king, also? Do not my warriors love me? Does the Moor hesitate to dye his sword with the blood of the Spaniard? Vizier, in half an hour let the troops be ready."

Silently but quickly the Vizier withdrew, and in less than half an hour the troops were collected. Boabdelin mounted his black Arab steed; the gates were opened silently, and the host of warriors marched out, more like a funeral procession than a military expedition. Like furious tigers they rushed upon the Spaniards, who, although they knew by experience the cunning of their foe, scarcely expected a sally from a weary and defeated enemy. The drums beat, the swords of the contending armies clashed together, and the roar of the cannon thundered through the night, and was echoed from the summits of the Alpuxares. But the Spaniards soon

rallied, and succor having arrived from Santa Fe, preceded
by monks bearing the brilliant cross, they made a gallant
defence. The moon had just risen, and as her peaceful light
shone over the scene, the groans of the wounded and the
dying mingled with the war-cries of the battle, and the waves
of the Xenil ran purple with gore as it rolled the blood of the
slain to the waters of the Guadalquiver. Boabdelin had
calculated justly; the reception which he had given to the
Christian monarch was a terrible one; and though the Saracens retired to the town after six hours' obstinate combat,
they had freed themselves from the stain on their honor and
reanimated their sinking courage.

CHAPTER II.

In a room, situated on the ground floor of an old house
which stood in one of the narrowest and most secluded streets
of the besieged town, sat the venerable Nissa. The appearance
of the apartment indicated the poverty of the inmates, but its
cleanliness was so striking that even a stranger would have
immediately perceived that the delicate hand of woman was
there. The floor was of dazzling whiteness; the walls were
covered with plaster of Paris, on which the remnants of some
arabesque painting were still dimly perceptible, and from the
ceiling hung a bright metal lamp with seven branches. An
old-fashioned chest of drawers seemed to contain the linen
and few valuables of the inmates, and under it lay several
rolls of parchment and some large volumes—a rare possession
indeed, at a time when the scarcity of books rendered them of
greater value. On a divan covered with red velvet reposed a
lovely maiden of eighteen, resting after the terror and disturb-
ance of the night. Her father, upon whom her eyes were
often turned with tender affection, was seated in his arm-chair
before the table, which was covered with books. Misfortune
had changed the color of his hair to grey in early years; his
eyes were dimmed with study, watching and tears; yet his
forehead was untouched by wrinkles, and his whole bearing

showed that his mind was peaceful and contented. Though he had not yet numbered sixty years, one would have taken him for a man who still preserved some of his youthful vigor, but who drew near to the closing scenes of life; and his long beard added still more to his reverend appearance.

"You are quite fatigued, Dinah," said he to the maiden; "the occurrences of the night have agitated you, although we ought to have become accustomed to these tumults. It is dreadful when Ishmael wars with Esau, but even more dreadful when they are at peace, and Israel becomes the victim of their truce. These scenes of war are nothing new to me, for I have known more horrible ones. Wandering on the banks of the Rhine, in my native Germany, I spent my youth. There every step was fraught with peril, for the common people were but the prey for which the nobles contended. When I grew up I longed to pray upon the ruins of the Temple, and turned my feet to the East, toward the land of my fathers; but that was no suitable spot for prayer; the wild Arabs drove the pilgrim far away, as if they envied him the melancholy pleasure of dropping a tear to the misery of his nation. I returned to my native country, and there met your mother. We were united, and you became the comfort of our distressed life. At that time the flower of our schools had been transplanted from the banks of the Tigris and Euphrates into this blessed country of the West. Here our thirst for knowledge might be satisfied; here, it was said, we might give our undisturbed attention to the study of the law, and to researches into the divine works. I left my home with you and your mother, and repaired to Sephrad. Sixteen years have passed away since then. Man has a country which he may call his own, the fox has a den, and the wild dove a nest, to which they may flee, but the only resting place of Israel is the grave. The wrath of the Lord has not ceased from his children. Soon will the cross be triumphant here, and we shall be deprived of even this repose."

He rose, and lifting his eyes to heaven, said: "Selima, blessed Selima! well have I guarded this jewel of yours—far more than the apple of mine eye. Even now I grieve in soul to see her want."

"Father," interrupted Dinah gently, "can you forget the words of the Psalmist? 'I have been young and am now old, yet have I not seen the righteous forsaken, nor his seed seeking bread.' Or those of the Prophet: 'Can a woman forget her sucking child, that she should not have compassion on the son of her sorrow? Yea, they may forget; yet will I not forget thee'?"

She rose and clasped her tender arms around the neck of her parent.

"Want, father, is the lot of the Jews; patiently must we endure our earthly sufferings, though they rob us of our most cherished blossoms. But see how brightly the morning sun shines into our humble chamber."

"Yes, my child," answered Nissa; "it shines on the earth, though it is stained with the blood of the slain; but its rays also fall on a scene of filial affection and submissive humility. Come, let us praise the Lord for his goodness."

And, turning toward the rising luminary, the two offered their morning prayers in quiet and solemn devotion.

This pious act was interrupted by a noise which began to prevail in the streets. The night sally had obtained for the Saracens a considerable amount of provisions, the distribution of which Boabdelin himself regulated. But not even the presence of the commander of the faithful was able to check the disorder of the famished people, who seized on the prey with avidity, and neither yielded to threats of the soldiers nor listened to the commands of their superiors. But the greater part of the Jewish inhabitants must long before have perished of hunger, had it not been for the caution of their elders, who, foreseeing the coming evil, had gathered together large stores of provisions, which they heaped up in their synagogues and schools. Every place became a storehouse; the ark itself was not exempt, and the scrolls of the law had their places supplied by loaves of bread. From these stores the poor people were supplied, and they had the satisfaction of knowing that there was still enough for a considerable time. Meanwhile they took the precaution of sending ragged Jews to every distribution of bread, and these feigned extreme grief when they got nothing but mockery and insult. The people, however, began at last to grow suspicious of the security in which the Jews seemed to live, and to wonder why so little distress was seen among them. The victory of the preceding evening had again roused the insolence of the people, and they were bent upon discovering what were the secret resources of the Jews.

One of the officers of the community had just turned the corner into the street in which Nissa lived, and bore concealed under his cloak some provisions which he had to bring to the poor man, who, though a foreigner by birth, was much venerated for his piety and learning. But a crowd of the lowest rank attacked him. Tearing open his cloak, they discovered the concealed food, and instantly demanded, with loud cries, first, half, and then the whole of what he carried.

"I am taking this to an old man of great learning," said the messenger; "the Cadi himself has given it to me for him. Cease, then, I pray you, and do not draw down on yourselves the wrath of the Lord."

But their cries became still more furious, and a Moor of the vilest class sprang forward, and brandished his cimeter over the head of the trembling man. Another one was just about to snatch the prey, when Dinah rushed from the house, followed by her terrified parent. Her exquisite beauty and unexpected boldness startled the ruffians for a moment, and she turned toward the messenger, seized the gift, and grasping one loaf firmly, threw the rest among the crowd, while she dragged the officer into the house at the same time. Like starving wolves, the people rushed upon the bread, and as they fought with each other for possession, Nissa, with his daughter and the alms-bearer, took refuge in the house, the door of which they secured behind them.

"Since the siege of Jerusalem," began the messenger, after a pause, "such horrors have never been witnessed; and surely, most venerable Nissa, had it not been for the obligations I am under to you for the instruction of my son, I should not have ventured on this errand. This is the third time I have been attacked on my way. Where is this to end? If they once discover our stores, our community can have no hope of escape."

"The Lord will save Israel from all his troubles,"
answered Nissa; "it would be better for us to perish, than to
fall into the hands of the Christians."

"You have an admirable daughter, father Nissa," said
the alms-bearer. "Though she be of German origin, yet she
excels the daughters of Sephrad both in beauty and virtue.
Young woman" continued he, "your duty is laborious, but it
is one of the sweetest kind; and since you honor your father,
your days will abound in happiness, for the divine promises
never fail. But, hark! the artillery of the Spaniards tells us
that the bloody work is once more begun. Surely Esau never
rests!

CHAPTER III.

During this time measures were being taken in the Spanish
camp to avenge the defeat, which they had suffered before
the eyes of their monarch.

The royal couple had visited the field of battle, accompanied by General Gonsalvo of Cordova, who listened with a
heavy heart to the reproaches for carelessness which the King,
to the joy of the attendant monks, showered upon him. The
cannon were again directed toward the town, and made considerable havoc among some prominent buildings, which had
once been Christian churches, but were then converted into
mosques. An assault was determined on. On the one hand
the miners cut their way under ground to the doomed city,
and, on the other, battalions were drawn out, ready to repulse
any sally of the besieged.

But all the efforts of the Spaniards were frustrated by the
valor of the Moors, who, being refreshed by the provision
they had taken, and reanimated by success, constructed
trenches behind the walls, and repelled the attacks of the
Spaniards with obstinacy and vigor. Their arrows also did
great execution, and many a Spanish youth was struck down
in the midst of the ranks by their deadly shafts.

Saddened by such sights as these, Ferdinand and Isabella
returned to their tent, absorbed in melancholy reflections,

and in this mood were they found by Thomas of Torquemada, who had entered the royal apartment. The aspect of this man was anything but pleasing; he was one of those who are never seen to smile, and his keen black eyes were shaded by bushy eyebrows, and a forehead contracted and wrinkled. Yet calm and collected as was his appearance, the close observer could detect, from the convulsive motion of his lips when he was speaking, that this serenity was but a mask under which he endeavored to conceal the strong and agitating feelings which filled his thoughts.

"Perchance this is an unfit time for an intrusion, Sire," said he, as he entered the tent.

"Nay," answered the King, "the guardian of our faith the Grand Inquisitor, can ever claim an audience from the kings of Arragon and Castile. Because upon this, our faith depends the power of the throne and the glory of Spain. Are we wanting in faith, holy father?"

"Faith is a cold and death-like thing, Sire, if it have not zeal to animate it. But to the purpose of my coming: It is in vain, great King, that the flower of our youth is sacrificed in this Moorish war, for the rust which cankers the Spanish arms is deeply seated in your own dominions. Vain will it be to implore the assistance of the Savior against the Infidels, if we suffer heresy to remain unchecked among us." Ferdinand's looks here betrayed curiosity and suspense. "I am informed by the Inquisitors of Seville," continued the priest, "that among the communities who have hypocritically assumed the name of Christians, numbers of abominable Marannos have been discovered. These persons profess our holy religion merely as a mask, under which they may carry out their disgraceful designs with impunity. They have been observed practising heretical ceremonies at the Feast of Dedication; they have been reading their blasphemous books on the Jewish Sabbath; the scarfs which they use in their worship have been found concealed in their dwellings; fathers even have been heard instructing their children in the principles of a false creed; and, to crown all, they have burnt the consecrated wafer, insulted the holy cross, and finally hid the image of the Anointed One in secret places, in order that they may there insult and mock it."

"But the proofs," said Isabella, whose zeal had been excited to frenzy; "have you the proofs of these crimes?"

"Can such horrors escape the keen eyes of the Church? Will not the oath of a Christian far outweigh the denials of the Marannos? Punishments, not proofs, are the objects of our thoughts; the time is short, and if we delay we must tremble lest the vengeance of heaven should fall heavily and yet justly on heedless Spain."

The royal pair became silent and thoughtful, and the Grand Inquisitor, following up the impression which he perceived he had made, thus continued :

"Murmurs are spreading among the people, and we must be careful lest the contagion should attack the army also. These heretical branches drain away all the sap of the noble tree of the Catholic religion, and it is only the arm of the Church which can root them up."

"What, then, do you ask of me?" demanded Ferdinand. "If I have rendered your arm so powerful, why need you my advice?"

Torquemada felt the reproof, but skilfully answered : "Because, Sire, the justice of the King should be united with the power of the Church. What I therefore ask of you is, that you, as a ruler of Arragon and Castile, will issue commands for the celebration of a solemn Auto-da-Fe in this very place, in order that by it we may avert the wrath of the Deity, fill the hearts of the soldiers with new spirits; and impress the Moors with the fear of punishment for their obstinate resistance. What! shall any King but a Christian fill the throne of the Spaniards? Shall any but the voices of true believers be heard in the Christian temples?" And turning confidentially to the King: "Believe me, Sire, the time is pressing, for there are many rebellious nobles leagued with these Moors and Marannos, who look with jealousy on your increasing power and would gladly aid that defeat which would alter their humble position."

These last words decided the King, and a proclamation of an Auto-da-Fe was accordingly made to the army amid universal applause.

CHAPTER IV.

While the numerous and desperate sallies of the Moors, and the breaches which were daily made in the intrenchments, kept the Spanish soldiers in employment, the carpenters on their part were busied in erecting a lofty scaffold immediately before the gates of Santa Fe. The workmen, heated with Madeira and Xeres, worked as swiftly and cheerily as if they were building a throne for the King. The lofty pile gradually rose up, composed of beams of wood, the interstices of which were filled with straw or hay, while a brick wall surrounded the whole. The soldiers, when relieved from duty, flocked around as spectators, and numbers of the country people offered their aid, both in the actual building and in the transportation of the necessary timber from the neighboring mountains. Around the wall they dug a ditch, which was again surrounded by an iron chain, so as to leave but one narrow entrance to the center. But the reader will ask the purpose of such a work. Was it a building to terrify the besieged? No. The timbers were destined to be consumed by fire even hotter than the beams of the Spanish sun, for this was the spot on which more than 1,000 unfortunate Marannos were destined to perish in the flames. This was the temple which the Spaniards erected in honor of that Being whom men call their Father, and this was the altar for the sacrifice. Here was the wood and the stone, but where was the lamb for a burnt offering?

A mournful cavalcade of victims now approached from Seville, surrounded by an immense concourse of people. In a long train of carts were numbers of reverend looking old men, whose limbs were loaded with chains, and whose avert look indicated fear and suspense. Behind them men, women, and children, were goaded along by the soldiery, as if they had been sheep. Truly it was a sight of misery. Here might be heard the loud screams of one, and there might you see another shedding tears of silent sorrow, while the cries of the poor victims, as they begged for one drop of water, were sorrowful in the extreme. Some of them became almost frantic with fatigue, and one man was so maddened by despair that he seized the lance which a soldier carried, and having first slain with it his wife, his child and the soldier, plunged it in his own heart.

"Glory to the Lord and death to the Marannos!" "Praise the Lord, for His mercy endureth forever!" Such were the exclamations of the soldiers and their captives as they took their path to the camp.

They had now arrived before the gates of Santa Fe, where amid the Spanish camp towered the lofty pile. But one night's repose was accorded to the victims, for darkness now drew her veil around the earth, the twinkling stars shone out in the silent heavens, all unmoved by the tumults of the world, and the planets rolled on in their eternal circles, unstayed by the wishes of an earthly king. The sun sunk down to rest, to give his light to the people of the other hemisphere, where the spirit of war had not as yet penetrated, and where happiness and peace still reigned triumphant; unconsicous of the ruin soon to overtake them.

On the following day an immense multitude was assembled before the camp, and the sight was rendered most imposing by the number of soldiers in their brightest armor, and the train of monks who bore the sacred cross. The walls of Granada were crowded with spectators. A gallery had been erected around the scaffold, and was thronged with persons who awaited the spectacle with feelings of pleasure. Among these the king was seen standing upon a balcony and receiving the cheers of his subjects. Torquemada then ascended the tribunal, and, amidst profound silence, began an address. In order to suppress compassion in the hearts of the bystanders he reproached the unhappy victims with their crimes, telling them they had previously forfeited, by their sins, the grace shown to them on their admission into the bosom of the Church, and exhorting them, by repentance before death escape eternal punishment. The pile was then fired; flames flashed upward into the bright sky, and wreaths of smoke burst forth from every part. The victims were driven toward the burning furnace. Some, with hymns and hosannahs on their lips, folded their children in their arms and walked calmly to the place of execution; some sued in vain for mercy at the pitiless soldiers, who heeded not their protestations of repentance, but drove them onward to the fire ; while others, furious with despair, struggled with their executioners only to meet with death from their ready swords, and to be cast lifeless into the flames.

Half an hour passed away ; the moans and shrieks of the dying were hushed in the silence of death ; but the flames burnt on, and the shouts of the multitude were still heard as they lingered around the spot, until the chiming of the evening bells called them to repose.

CHAPTER V.

The priest had made his calculations well. The besiegers fought with redoubled courage, indefatigable perseverance, and admirable bravery. Some few ramparts were yet to be taken, some few points to be weakened, and an assault might then admit them into the city. But the sword and cannon of the Spaniards were not their only armament, for famine was within the city, and all its horrors followed in its train. Nevertheless the pride of the Moorish King was not yet humbled. He saw his fate approach, but he sought to meet it bravely.

Nissa lay on a sick bed, and his beloved daughter sat by him, clasping the hand of her suffering father. Her eyes filled with tears as she looked on his suffering frame and felt the quick throbbing of his fevered pulse. For two days the alms-bearer had not been there. Half a loaf and a bottle of wine were now all the provisions left to sustain the suffering man and his fair attendant. On this morning she had left the house for a short time while her father slept, and had hastened to the great Synagogue, where the emaciated forms of her co-religionists besought heaven for the deliverance of the town. It was no surprise to the assembled company to behold a female appearing on such a day within the sacred walls, and throwing herself at the feet of the chief Rabbi to beg assistance for her poor father. In times of distress like this, man forgets the petty laws which he has imposed upon himself, and clings to the simple and eternal truths of his Heavenly Father. The venerable Rabbi went to the Ark, and taking the rest of the wine over which the benediction had been pronounced, he gave it to the lonely supplicant, accompanying the gift with the words : " This is all that the Saracens have left us ; may it be like the holy bottle of oil which Judas Maccabæus found in a polluted temple, and which, small as it was, furnished the lamp for eight days. May this wine refresh the pious sufferer, and be never consumed until deliverance be granted unto Israel, or until he enjoy a far different life in those realms of happiness where war can never harm us, where distress can never enter." With this gift she had returned home.

A storm had been gathering during the morning, and now it broke over the city. The thunders of the cannon were unheard amid those of the Almighty. Peal after peal sounded through the sky and found an answer in the echoes of the mountains. The air was darkened, the lightning flashed, and the little chamber was filled with the glare. Nissa awoke.

" Thou who hast taken me from the womb of my mother, enlighten my dark path," said he to himself. " My dear Dinah, the Messiah is coming."

Dinah thought he spoke these words deliriously, and looked timidly at him.

"The Messiah is coming to-day, my daughter. Death is the Messiah, and he will free us from all our troubles and lead us to a new and blissful life. The Messiah is the Savior who will lead me on my way. 'Thou wilt show me the path of life ; in thy presence is fulness of joy ; at thy right hand are pleasures forever more.'"

The thunder here broke in a crash over the house, and Dinah knelt down on the floor and offered up an ardent prayer.

"Dinah," said Nissa, in a broken voice, "there is not a mosque, a church, or a synagogue, which has ever heard a prayer like that within its walls. Truly the breast of a pure maiden is the most solemn sanctuary. Courage, then, my daughter; for, when all is fair and prosperous, it is an easy thing to be calm and collected; but to stand fast and enured in the days of trial, this indeed is the work only of religion."

Exhausted by speaking, he fell back on the couch; but after some moments' rest he resumed: "Before the thundering heavens and the trembling earth, before the Great Invisible, I deliver into your hands five inestimable treasures, far excelling all the riches of the world: I leave with you your innocent heart, your maiden honor, the holy religion of our forefathers, the memory of your parents, and your own fate. An hour shall come when you will be asked whether these jewels have been kept or lost; and when it comes the memory of this hour will rise with it. Then, my daughter, shall I stand with you before the throne of our Great Father; then shall I be asked if this be the same spotless girl whom I left on earth. Oh, let me pray that you may not be altered, but that, pure as ever, I may recognize you again; for then shall be rewarded all the toils of life; then shall be realized all my hopes of the future. But, hark! the messenger of God approaches."

A terrific clap was heard. The sufferer began to struggle with death. His breath became heavier and shorter; his look more staring; a cold perspiration stood in drops upon his brow, and his pulse grew fainter and fainter still. Dinah wrung her hands in despair. Not even the brethren, whose custom it was to visit the death-bed and cheer the dying with prayers and consolation, not even they were there. Each was at home in the misery of the time; each had to watch by some expiring relation. The weeping daughter clasped her hands and embraced her father, as if to arrest the soul in its flight, but it was all in vain. Nissa faintly murmured out, "And when Jacob had made an end of commanding his sons, he gathered up his feet into the bed and yielded up his soul, and was gathered unto his people." And then, a few minutes afterward, he said: "Hear, O Israel, the Lord our God is one God."

A few moments more and all was still, for the spirit of Nissa had returned to the God who gave it, and Dinah was alone in the world.

CHAPTER VI.

The Spanish grandees were collected in the ante-chamber of the King, discussing the approaching capture of Granada. Mortars had been set in operation against the Alhambra, the ancient palace of the Moorish kings, and the terror which prevailed there might be distinctly seen from the Spanish camp. The Gothic windows were broken, the roof was destroyed, and the banner of the Prophet, which had once so proudly floated from the turrets, was now thrown down. The following night had been fixed upon for a general assault.

In one corner of the chamber stood Torquemada, Ximeres, and other priests, engaged in a lively conversation about the territories around Granada, which had, 900 years before, belonged to the Church; and a Franciscan monk was relating the manner in which the Moors had gained possession of the Spanish soil, and how they had, by treason, increased and extended their power.

One man, however, stood aloof from these groups. Distinguished by his figure and the nobility of his bearing, he paced the hall with lengthened strides, silent and apparently absorbed in thought. The rest seemed to take no notice of him, except to cast a glance of scorn or envy. This person was robust, his cast of features serious, and his forehead high; his hair was simply arranged, and a Spanish cloak was wrapped loosely around his shoulders. Though he did not join in the conversation of any of the groups, he occasionally stopped and listened to some of their remarks. This man was Don Isaac Abarbanel, Privy Councillor to the King of Arragon. At last he was addressed by Ximenes:

"How many does your community in Granada number, Don Isaac?"

"I know not," replied the Councillor, stopping; "I have never been in this part of the country."

"How comes it that you, the greatest Jew in Arragon, have no information about this?" remarked Torquemada.

"The number of Jews and Moors in Granada matters little to me, worthy father; the King's service alone occupies my attention."

At this moment a page entered to summon Don Isaac to the royal apartment, into which he was immediately conducted.

Ferdinand addressed him in a cheerful tone:

"I have ordered you to our headquarters, my friend, because, as you well know, your presence is most important to me."

The Councillor bowed. "Any ability which I may have is ever at the service of your Majesty."

"Do you think the royal treasury will gain by the capture of Granada?"

"My King's kindness will gain him as many faithful subjects as Granada numbers inhabitants. It will be but of little consequence to the Moors by whom they are governed. If your Majesty's clemency leaves them their mosques, they will then pay taxes to you as willingly as they did to Boabdelin."

"This may be true; but the treasury of the Moorish King is, I suppose, well stocked?"

"If he has not already sent the greater part to Africa. If the capture of the city could be effected quickly, more might be expected."

"How many does your community in Granada number, Abarbanel?"

"My King's servant does not know; but the greater part of them are learned men."

"Who are at the same time rich," added Ferdinand, smiling. "The Spanish Jews unite riches with learning, the most illustrious example of which I now see before me."

Abarbanel bowed. "My knowledge is worth little, my royal master, if it does not suffice for the service of my King."

"We have need of money, Don Isaac. The long siege has exhausted our finances, both of Arragon and Castile; and besides, we have been paying double money to the soldiers for the last eight days. We will therefore, if possible, make this night the conclusion of this sanguinary conflict. I intend to make you Minister of Finance for the newly gained provinces. Could you furnish my treasury, to-day, with fifty thousand piasters?"

Abarbanel meditated for a moment. "Certainly," said he, "they are at thy royal service."

"Take with you the assurance of my favor," said the King, "and to-morrow I hope we shall meet each other in the Alhambra."

A page entered to announce an embassy from the Moorish King, and Abarbanel quitted the chamber, leaving the King in apparently good spirits.

CHAPTER VII.

In the great hall stood the thrones of Ferdinand and Isabella. The pillars which supported the roof were twined with laurel and velvet tapestry. Above the throne were the arms of Arragon and Castille, worked in gold, and between them hung a golden crucifix, ornamented with diamonds. All around stood the priests in their black, and the chancellors in their white robes, and a large concourse of nobles in brilliant armor were already assembled. The noise of the cannon had ceased, and only the murmurs of the camp at Santa Fe were heard without.

The Duke of Medina-Sidonia now introduced Boabdelin's ambassadors. They were fine, tall men, attired in sky-blue caftans; at their sides hung their short swords, ornamented with jewels, and their heads were covered with turbans studded with precious stones. About an hour passed away in solemn and anxious silence. At length Ferdinand entered, leading in his consort, the Queen of Castile, and they took their seats upon the thrones. The embassy were summoned to approach, and Mustapha, an aged man, began to speak:

"Christian monarch," said he, "the Lord of heaven and earth, the Lord of war and peace, has given the victory into your hands. This day is the anniversary of the battle of Xeres, when we first obtained that home in this land which we have maintained for 870 years. Much blood has been spilt between our forefathers. Often has the valor of the nations, both of the East and of the West, been proved by their illustrious deeds. But we have also transplanted the arts of peace to this happy land, and whilst other countries have been overwhelmed in the darkness of ignorance, we have nourished the

light of science and communicated it to our Christian neigh-
bors. But, alas! the brightness of those days is vanished.
Your valor, gallant King, and your prudence, august Queen,
have obtained the victory. Our empires have long since been
annihilated. Granada is the only monument which yet tells
of our former greatness; and we are now ready to open her
gates, trusting that the royal ruler will not, by too great
harshness, abuse the power which the Lord has put into his
hands."

After some consultation with the Chancellor, the King
thus addressed the Ambassadors:

"It was not by their bravery alone that your ancestors
conquered the Spanish soil; it was by base treason that they
opened the gates of cities and snatched the arms from the
hands of our gallant ancestors. But see the way of avenging
Providence: On the anniversary of that sanguinary battle
you are standing before the thrones of Arragon and Castille,
suing for mercy. You may speak of your opening the gates
of your city, but even were you not to do it we should have
forced our way in before the sun rose again upon us. We are
well aware that you have to contend, not only against the
Spanish arms, but against the plagues of heaven, hunger and
pestilence as well. We are well aware that the Moors bear
with reluctance the yoke of Boabdelin, and are already revolt-
ing against him. Nevertheless we are still ready to receive
you as our subjects, if this day the keys of the town and castle
be delivered to us, and if Boabdelin renounce that title and
authority of King which becomes only Christian monarchs."

Meanwhile Torquemada had invited them to his residence,
and whilst there he artfully represented to them the gracious-
ness of his King, and gave them to understand that the depo-
sition of Boabdelin was the chief thing which he wished, and
that they would be allowed to retain liberty of worship and an
administration according to their own laws. He seemed to be
better acquainted with the situation of Granada than even the
King, and he employed all his priestly artifice to induce them
to revolt against their unfortunate monarch. The Moors had,
within the last few years, been torn by domestic contention,
and the kings had been rapidly changed, one being expelled

by another. Boabdelin alone had succeeded in securing their
fidelity, and reconciling all parties to each other, by his own
virtues. But a war of eleven years duration had now wearied
the nobles, and they thought that beneath the Christian king's
government they might uninterruptedly enjoy the possession
of those riches which they had gathered from the general
wreck. Freedom of worship and administration according to
their own laws were, in their opinion, too precious to be
endangered by fruitless obstinacy. Though they could not
suppress a feeling of fear and shame when they thought of
Boabdelin, yet they also knew that the famished population
were anxiously expecting deliverance, and that it would be
easy to get rid of a monarch who was already forsaken by all.
Relying on Torquemada's promises, they agreed to surrender
the city early next morning, if those promises were confirmed
by Ferdinand, and if the dethroned monarch received a
pension suitable to his rank. A few hours afterward, a Domin-
ican priest brought them the document, to which the royal
seal was affixed. The peace was confirmed and the Ambassadors returned to Granada.

CHAPTER VIII.

Boabdelin listened in silence to the Ambassadors, as they
represented to him the conditions.

" You have done well," said he; " but you will be surprised
to find in what way the Christian prince will keep his word.
Do not ask me to sign the treaty. Is this the fidelity which
you owe to me? Do you believe in a Moorish Empire without
a Moorish King?"

They represented to him again their terrible situation, and
assured him that if a spark of hope were left they had rather
be buried beneath the ruins of Granada than submit to a
Christian conqueror. Boabdelin stopped, and taking their
hands he shook them, saying, with a noble resignation:

" Well, be it so then. Open the gates to-morrow morning.
But I will not trust to Christian mercy; I shall leave before
their entrance, and seek beyond the sea a refuge from the
King's enmity. I thank you for your services. Farewell."

Sadly the grandees left the palace, and the banners of peace soon floated from every part of the walls. Strife was ended, and in the Spanish camp they held feasts of joy. But who can describe the feelings of Boabdelin? Night had spread its veil upon the horizon, and he rose from the couch where he had lain a short while. The Alhambra, yesterday so lively, was now wrapped in deep silence, for solitude and desolation reigned throughout it. Looking forth upon the spreading landscape, "Oh, my country," said he, " thou hast cost me tears and blood; thou hast robbed me of the flower of my youth ; but thou hast not despoiled me of my peace of mind."

Such were his proud reflections ; but when he looked toward the Spanish camp, and saw the fires which had been kindled in expression of their joy ; when he heard the shouts of the people as they longed for the morrow, which was to give them bread; when he looked around on his spacious palace, and met not a single smile of pleasure, not a single look of friendship; when he thought how, on the morrow, the hated Ferdinand would celebrate his triumph on that very spot, whilst he himself must abandon the kingdom of his fathers ; when he cast his thoughts back to the days of his youth, when he and his mother languished in the dungeon into which they had been thrown by the second Christian consort of his father; when his looks fell on the mosques, which were soon to receive Christian monks—when he thought of all these things, of his rival's happiness and his own misery, he could bear it no longer, but, covering his face with his hands, gave free vent to the tears of despair. He soon recovered himself, however, and seizing a phial which he had kept about him for a long time, he swallowed the contents at a draught, and sat down on his divan to await the fatal consequences. But the poison was too much weakened by age to take its usual effect, and the strength of his constitution, combined with the efforts of his old physician, who was called in, were successful in counteracting the poison, and a profound sleep fell upon him. When he awoke the morning was dawning, the drums of the Spanish army were heard, the troops stood before the gates, and the last of the Moorish monarchs was conducted by a few faithful servants on board a ship, which immediately set sail for Africa.

At the gates the Moorish authorities received the victorious Spaniards. The entrance of the army lasted the whole day, and the inconstant multitude greeted the victors with loud shouts, especially Ferdinand and Isabella, who could now justly call themselves the monarchs of Spain. A long train of wagons laden with provisions satisfied the hunger of the conquered, and in a few hours the bazaar was again full of life, and the streets were crowded with people engaged in familiar conversation. The camp was broken up and the warlike instruments conveyed to the town; the Court took posession of the Alhambra, and the effects of a war that had lasted nine years seemed to be obliterated by one day of peace. And when, in the evening, an illumination took place, and *Te Deums* were chanted in the public square and masses celebrated, one would have imagined that tranquility had returned to the town. But it was with envious looks and frantic rage that the priests saw the Mussulmen, confiding in the royal word, seek their mosques as was their wont—for they considered that it was no real conquest while God was worshiped with infidel ceremonies. The call to prayer from the minarets wounded their pride, and the Imans, in their long robes, became the butts of their wit and the objects of their execrations. Even Ferdinand regretted that he had purchased Granada at so high a price.

Scarcely had a few weeks elapsed before a convention of the Clergy, under Torquemada's guidance, was called to deliberate upon the religious affairs of the new subjects. The mind of the President, ever intent upon acts of violence, had great influence, and the wily priest induced the wavering spirits of the others to declare the memorable words, that "*A Christian monarch is not bound to keep his word with Infidels.*" Orders were immediately given to close the mosques; the Ulemas were forbidden, under penalty of death, to hold any meeting for religious purposes, and they were commanded to burn their books.

The people were struck with amazement, which was soon followed by general excitement. But this had been expected, and even wished for. Precautionary measures had been taken, and when the Moors attempted to force open the mosques, and, with the few arms that had been left them, to commence a revolt, soldiers occupied every house, cannons were drawn up in every street, the rebels were driven back like a flock of sheep, and compelled to choose between exile and Christianity. Many thousands preferred the former, following their King to Africa. But many assumed, apparently, the creed of the Christian, keeping strictly to their own tenets, while many fell in despair beneath the swords of the Spaniards.

Thus ended the empire of the Moors in Spain. The country lost its most illustrious inhabitants, and the people were bereft of their long untarnished glory.

CHAPTER IX.

In the apartment assigned to him by the King in Granada, Don Isaac Abarbanel was engaged in conversation with his son Jehuda, a youth of noble mind and bearing. As he had been educated with the sons of the nobility, his manners had received the mould of the Spanish grandees, but his youthful mind when placed in these favorable circumstances, took but a superficial view of things, and looked more on the bright than on the dark side of life. Persevering and varied study had given to the father all the gravity of age, but the son was more conversant with the sweet poetry and light literature of the time, and thus but touched the subjects he studied, culling only the pleasant part of them, and flitting, like the butterfly, from flower to flower. The father was moved by the misery of his people. He had seen disaster approaching with giant strides, and had left his peaceful home and the leisure of private life in order to stay its progress, and, from a more elevated position, to be more capable of relieving it. In this he had succeeded. He had rendered himself indispensable to Ferdinand and Isabella in the financial department, although he was not strong enough to rescue from destruction the proselytes whom he would, perhaps, have left to ruin if he had possessed the power of saving them, hating them for deserting the faith of their fathers. The son, on the other hand, held many views entirely different from those of his father, for he felt the inconvenience which his faith imposed upon him, and though he would never have thought of abandoning it during Don Isaac's life, he attached no importance to religion, and much less did he think of performing strictly all the religious ceremonies of the Jews.

"Have you seen the elders of the community, my son? Have you inquired into all their wants?"

"I have told them to come to you, my father; but I do not wish to waste my time with such trifling matters."

"Trifling matters they may seem to you, but you cannot waste your time more than you do wandering with your friend Alonzo about the streets playing the guitar."

"Do not reprove me, father," said Jehuda. "If I could purchase the liberty of my co-religionists with my heart's blood, if my life were required to obtain it, I would give it willingly; but to struggle on, step by step, meeting new difficulties every minute—to quarrel about an old synagogue with priests and monks, who are ever ready to answer our assertions with their sophistry—to trouble about every trifle, and to feel oneself wounded by every attack, this I own is too great a thing for me, especially when I consider how unimportant is the result."

Abarbanel fixed his eye on the youth in astonishment. "Look, my son," said he, leading him to the window, where a fair prospect, enclosed by mountains, met the eye; "look at that weeping willow; its bending branches have for many years escaped the violence of the winds, storms, and tempests. It bends down, but the branches protect the stem. And now look at that sturdy oak which the storm has overthrown. Israel is like the willow, which bends before the storm but rises again when it is passed. By the existence of these trifling matters, as you call them, we withstand time and its tempests, and fulfil our mission of being a remnant of past ages, lasting for ever, and giving a proof to the nations of one true God. Thus the part which we act in history is not a bright but an everlasting one; it is a part not distinguished by earthly greatness, but wonderful to the mind. Thus it is that, though we are a nation, we do not form an empire among the nations—for we are the imperishable monuments of antiquity. Thousands of peoples have vanished; the empire of the Moors has been annihilated before our eyes, because it was a power of this world and obstinately resisted existing things; but we stand for ever, and yield patiently to the oppression that cannot destroy us."

"I yield to the noble sentiments of my father, for I would not embitter one moment of his dear life; but I love life and all its brightness."

"Oh that it may be ever bright to you. But a time will arrive when it will become more serious. Nevertheless, what you will not do in the name of religion do in the name of humanity. Conduct the elders to me. Here are several petitions from those who have become impoverished during the siege, and especially this one from the orphan daughter of a German sage. You can attend to the case yourself, for the means of succor are at your disposal."

CHAPTER X.

Jehuda left his father wrapt in thought. His observation was but too just. For friendship, for liberty, for his country, he would willingly have sacrificed his life; but his inexperienced mind could not comprehend how his father, honored by the King and endeared to the nobility, could weaken his influence by perpetual intercessions for his co-religionists, especially when his efforts in their behalf were repaid by many of them with envy and ingratitude. He thought that were it not for this whimsical ardor Abarbanel might occupy a still more illustrious position, and lead a life more free from anxiety. It was this very anxiety about others that disturbed his free and careless mind. He looked over the papers which his father had handed him, and determined first to visit the youthful Jewess, who had been so particularly recommended to him. Accordingly he set out immediately. He had gone but a few paces on his way when he met his friend Alonzo.

Descended from a noble but impoverished family, Alonzo had become an officer in the King's service, and given himself up to the careless enjoyment of life, but was nevertheless of the same liberal and generous mind as his friend, with whom he had been educated at Lisbon by a kind relative, who had taken charge of him when left a helpless orphan. On the romantic banks of the Tejo their hearts had been open to one another, and had become linked in the ties of eternal friendship. Alonzo, though remembering with pleasure his noble birth, was far above regarding petty differences in rank or creed. With him the "Pater Noster" of some burly priest called forth the same mockery as the mumbling of a Jewish Rabbi. Friendship, music and song were the objects which he valued most, and, imperceptibly, the same tastes sprung up in the mind of his friend. Sometimes they would share in the wild diversions of youth; but when they did so it was only in order to heighten the enjoyment of those calmer and more and similar noble which they sought in the study of nature healthy pleasures pursuits.

When they met, Alonzo had just returned from a banquet, given by some of his companions in arms. He was glad to have escaped from their noisy circle, and nothing more agreeable could have happened to him than to meet his friend.

"So thoughtful, Jehuda!"

"I am, to-day, my father's alms-bearer," answered Jehuda; "and when I peruse these petitions, it seems difficult to decide where the greatest distress prevails, and where succor should be first given. But I will give the preference to modesty joined to poverty, and visit first the writer of this letter. Will you accompany me?"

Alonzo willingly accompanied his friend. They soon found the house, entered the old apartment already known to the reader, and found Dinah absorbed in reading. As the young men entered her countenance at first became agitated, and then suffused with blushes. She soon, however, became reassured by the noble bearing of her visitors, although the inquietude of her heart might be perceived from the agitation and heaving of her bosom. The two young men were also struck.

There is not, indeed, a more affecting sight than sorrowing beauty; and of all the maidens whom they had seen in Spain, none had ever appeared to them half so lovely. The long mourning dress, and the curls flowing freely unconcealed, in Moorish fashion, increased their interest which her figure and features inspired, and set off the paleness with which suffering and want had tinged her countenance. Besides this, her occupation, which had been interrupted by the entrance of the young men, contributed to give her a noble expression; and, combined with this, her carriage was noble, commanding, and expressive of natural reserve.

"Pardon us, worthy maiden," began Jehuda, "if we have disturbed you in a holy occupation. I am sent here by my father, the Privy Councillor, Don Isaac Abarbanel, in order to relieve you from the sad situation in which you have been placed by the hand of destiny."

"Has the noble Senor, your worthy father, thought my request worthy such speedy consideration. Truly my gratitude cannot be greater than his liberality."

Juhuda felt at this moment that he would willingly have given up all the treasures of his father if he had been deserving of the praise which had been lavished upon his parent. And yet he felt a strange agitation within him, as it seemed to him that he was the suppliant, and the simple maiden before him the mistress of his fate. His looks wandered now to Alonzo, whose tearful eyes were fixed on the fair Jewess, and now to Dinah, who looked modestly on the floor. The characters of both the young men, though tinctured with levity, were yet uncorrupted; passion had not yet taught them to look with lecherous eyes on beauty, but both seemed equally struck, with this difference, that Alonzo stood immovable as a statue, while Jehuda could not conceal the agitation of his soul. A few moments of silence ensued, which Dinah first broke.

"During the siege I lost my father. A consumptive fever overcame his powerful constitution, and he who had sought in this country a peaceful home found only a grave. An old Moor who, during my father's life, often came to converse with him on astronomy, charged himself with his burial, and supported me as far as his means allowed. But he, too, did not survive the fall of his race. I am now alone, quite alone, without a friend or relation in the world. I am too young to depend on alms, and my sex forbids my hand-labor. What I should desire is a situation as governess for children, or duenna to some lady."

Tears abundantly poured down her cheeks as she spoke, and as the two young men looked at her, they thought they had never seen such a picture of dignity blended with melancholy.

"My father will take care of you," said Jehuda at length, stepping forward and seizing her hand. "Console yourself; Don Isaac Abarbanel is a father to the fatherless, and you will find in him a friend and adviser. Meanwhile accept this small gift, which will supply your most urgent wants, and to-morrow I shall see you again."

"But are you not afraid, fair maiden," said Alonzo, "living thus alone in Granada at such a troublous time? How easily might any accident happen to you and your friends not know anything of it."

"This street is secluded, this house is humble, and violence does not visit such dwellings. Nevertheless I am often afraid; but I put my trust in the Lord, for He who keepeth Israel neither slumbers nor sleeps."

"Would it not be better," interposed Jehuda, "if I were to conduct you to-day to my father's house, where you might live in security?"

For a moment Dinah knew not what to reply. "Senor," she said at length, "it is not without cause that Israel expects its deliverance through your noble family. Truly you are an excellent shoot of its branches. Truly, the Abarbanels are worthy of their ancestors. Thanks, most sincere thanks, for your kindness; but pray leave me for this day in mine own house, for it would be painful to leave the spot where my last hope expired. Bear my best greetings to Don Isaac Abarbanel."

The young men left the house and walked on in silence, for they had not yet learned to hide their feelings under the mask of indifference.

Jehuda spoke after a while: "A charming creature, this maiden."

"Uniting the dignity of woman with the spirit of man," replied Alonzo.

"My father must do something for her," said Jehuda. Alonzo gave no reply.

"A duenna!" continued the young man, "subjected to the whims of a nervous senora. No, never!" Alonzo could not answer but by sobs.

The two friends separated at the gate of Abarbanel's house, for each of them wished to be alone, in order to give themselves up to their own feelings. Had it not been so, they would have walked together in the orange groves on the banks of the Xenil, to pass the fine evening in friendly conversation. But Dinah stood at the window, watching the stars rise silently in the heavens, until her eyes were dazzled by their brightness, reflected in her tears. She then took her guitar and sung the following verses:

> Thou who mournest, cease to weep,
>   Dash the teardrop from thine eye;
> Soon shall death's unmoving sleep
>   Stifle every bitter sigh.
>
> Man is like a Summer flower,
>   Decked in every beauteous hue—
> Just as lovely for an hour,
>   Just as swiftly fading too.
>
> Yet full many a mournful tear
>   Dims this little space of life;
> Sad are all our moments here,
>   All our ways with grief are rife.
>
> Then when death our friends may sever,
>   Let not sorrow touch our breast;
> Soon, for ever and for ever,
>   We shall join them in their rest.

CHAPTER XI.

Don Isaac Abarbanel gave up his evenings to his favorite studies. There lay before him the Book of Books, the Book of Promises, the comfort of the faithful, which has for years inspired quiet and comfort in minds oppressed with misfortune. He had penetrated into the spirit of the writings as none before him had done, and, despising the useless controversies about the letter, he sought in the Scriptures the living principles of his ancestors. This manner of studying had imbued his mind with a dignity which rendered him capable of opposing the mean endeavors and cabals of the monks at Ferdinand's Court by an intellectual and moral conviction.

The best method of enduring the struggle into which wicked men enter for the sake of wealth, and to which the mind is allured by every kind of deceit, is to despise the conflict, to be prepared at every moment for the loss, and to value one's better part far more than is usually done. Thus it is that our life becomes at the same time an object and the means of attaining it.

The Book of Kings was on that day the object of Abarbanel's researches, for he loved to let his mind wander back to the glorious days of his nations independence, and to examine the causes of its fall. Beside this, as he could trace his pedigree back to the royal family of David, the chronicle of the ancient Kings became at the same time the chronicle of his family.

Jehuda entered and told his father of his visit to the fair orphan. With all the liveliness of his mind he described her beauty, her virtue, the cultivation of her mind, the distress of her situation, and, with all the glowing eloquence of youth, he asked for some extraordinary support for her and her reception to the house of his father.

"And how is it with the rest of the sufferers, my son?" asked Abarbanel.

Jehuda blushed and did not reply. The beauty of the maiden had driven all other thoughts from his mind, and he felt the reproof expressed in his father's look. It needed, indeed, not so much the penetration as that of the Privy Councillor to discover that the impression left on the mind of his son by the visit was somewhat deeper than simple compassion. Abarbanel was not free from a certain pride, characteristic of the Spanish Jews, which caused them to look down with a degree of contempt upon their co-religionists in France and Germany. It is true that the latter were, in some respects, of far inferior condition, from the continued series of misfortunes which their powerful enemies had brought upon them, and from the mockeries to which they were exposed by inferior antagonists. They had been both socially and morally neglected, and in them was fulfilled the word of Holy Writ: "And upon them that are left alive of you I will send a faintness into ther hearts in the land of their enemies, and the sound of a shaken leaf shall chase them, and they shall flee as falling from a sword, and they shall fall when none pursueth." Thus living in continual fear, deprived of the means of noble pursuits, and maintaining their lives by usury with the clergy and nobility, they did not follow those better and more eleva. ting literary pursuits which distinguished the Spanish Jews. Abarbanel therefore perceived with displeasure the impression which a German Jewess had made upon his son. Nevertheless he did not reproach him for having neglected the other sufferers, but listened attentively to his narrative and then formed his resolution. "Since your protege," said he, "is insured against urgent want, you may leave the rest to me." With these words he dismissed his son.

CHAPTER XII.

The streets of Granada were alive with bustle. The army had marched out for a review, the morning service was over the converted Moors were sitting in their shops awaiting customers, and the monks had left the newly established monasteries to collect the gifts offered by charity. At such an early hour on the following day, Abarbanel left the Synagogue of his Congregation even before the service was concluded. The poor persons standing at the gate made room for the

Privy Councillor, as they thankfully received the alms which he bestowed upon them, without looking either at the gift or the benefactor. Abarbanel then turned a corner and entered the well known street, and soon arrived at the house tenanted by Nissa's daughter. The door was fastened, and was opened only after repeated knockings. As soon as his eyes fell on Dinah, who met him with reverence, his son's conduct was no longer a riddle to him. Dinah seemed in no way embarrassed at the arrival of this venerable man, for his appearance was one from which good only could be augured. She had been occupied in arranging her father's papers, and at every new discovery her feelings overcame her, and her tears fell in floods as she pressed the dear relics to her heart.

"Do you search for an inheritance from your father, daughter of Nissa?"

"Oh, no, venerable senor; my inheritance is only [his memory, which lives for ever with me. But you cannot blame a weak mortal who treasures every little remnant of one who was dearly loved."

"The memory of the just is a blessing," remarked Abarbanel. "Do you know me, my daughter?"

"I never had the honor of seeing you, senor; but, if I mistake not, I see before me the noblest Israelite of the age, the Privy Councillor of the King, Don Isaac Abarbanel."

Abarbanel smiled. "You had visitors yesterday." Dinah blushed. "Two young men, one of whom was my son, had the commission to convince themselves whether the writer of a certain letter, addressed to me, corresponded with the unusual neatness of the hand-writing, You seem to know a good deal more than the generality of your country-women."

"The title I know I owe to my father; my education was the principal occupation of his life."

"How long have you lived in Spain?"

"From my second year, and I am now eighteen."

"So young, and yet so clever."

"So young, Senor, and yet so tried with sorrow."

"How did your father obtain his livelihood?"

"By copying scrolls of the law."

"A poor employment, indeed."

"It was productive enough to maintain us, and small enough to teach us moderation."

"You wish for a situation, do you not? I can procure you a very brilliant one. Will you be duenna for a princess?"

"By the God of my fathers, not for all the riches of the world! You cannot be in earnest, Senor; my faith is a sacred jewel."

"But you need not abandon that among the nobility."

"No indeed, Senor, I would not abandon it for all the pleasures of this earth. But I am a weak maiden, accustomed to the stillness of a domestic life, and the dangers which would surround me in such a situation are great; while the calling of the Israelite is seclusion and the practice of his religion. Could I fulfil this among the bustle of the world? Am I experienced enough to withstand all the allurements of greatness?"

Aberbanel was moved. He had merely made the offer as a trial. "You are a noble-minded girl," said he, "you shall not be a duenna. But you cannot refuse to come and dwell at my house; for there you can, undisturbed, cultivate your mind, you need not fear any restriction with respect to your religion. I see you are musical, and am need of such a being as you, for heaven has not granted me a daughter, and the wife of my youth lies buried in Lisabon."

The girl seemed embarrassed; she lost the calmness which she had, till then, maintained; but in a few minutes she recovered her composure and answered:

"I thank you, Senor; I thank you for your kindness, which is so abundant to every one, and which is the prop of our hopes. What happier lot could be mine than to live in your house, in the house of him who is the father to his persecuted nation! Pardon my gratitude, but I cannot now choose that abode; permit me to pass this year of mourning in the circle of a family where I am seperated from all that might bring me back too soon to the world and its charms, and where I can prepare myself for the happy days which I shall spend with you. I must first compose myself, and become distinctly aware of my duties."

Abarbanel, who had not expected this, turned the conversation so different topics. He inquired after her acquaintances and she mentioned the name of an old physician, a friend of her fathers, with whom she would wish to reside. Abarbanel untertook himself to provide all that she required, and it was settled that she should seek her new abode the following day.

CHAPTER XIII.

At the break of day Don Alonzo had left his house and mounted his steed. Since the preceding evening his heart had been agitated by feelings never felt before, and for the first time he lost that cheerfulness which had, erewhile, accompanied him even in the most serious business of live. There was, however, a sweetness in the melancholy, which was so delicious that he would not have exhanged it for any joyful emotion. Absorbed in thought, he disregarded the beauty of the morning, and the sweet-smelling groves of orange trees, citrons and pomegranates, mingled with the exquisite-scented blossoms of the olive. His horse carried him to the ruins of the ancient city of Illiberis, from which a romatic path led to the rocky mountains. In this spot the eye is only here and there relieved by small patches of vendure. Masses of rock and ruined walls tower up in wild confusion, and flowers twine around the broken crags. Here, amid the ruins of human greatness, could he contemplate that prospect of the undying beauties of Nature, the sight of which ever calls to mind the littleness of human actions, when compared with the eternal works of the Creator, and while it teaches us to reflect seriously on ourselves, blends with the stern lesson the sweetest pleasures which can please our fancies, or captivate our minds.

Arrived at the ruins, Alonzo alighted, and having fastened the bridle of his horse to a bush of blooming bentiscus, sat down on some broken fragments, to revel in his own thoughts. His heart glowed within him, as his imagination dwelt upon the Jewish maiden, and pictured her every action adorned with joy, while he obtained for her, with his own hand, those pleasures which, though simple, were no less acceptable. To lead such a being from its isolation into a cheerful existence, to procure her a happiness which she had never before felt, to open for a beautiful mind the shrine of science and art, to show to a clear-sighted eye the beauties of nature, the reveal to the feeling heart the divinity of human virtue, of human friendship and love, and to make such a creature enter into the enjoyment of a new world—in short, to embellish another being with our own better nature; these are the desires which live only in a noble breast, and bear the stamp of true magnanimity and love.

It was now, for the first time, that Alonzo felt the pressure of poverty; before, he had been indifferent to earthly riches, now he ardently longed for them. It was true that his friend possessed them in abundance, and Alonzo had never hesitated to consider his friend's possessions as his own, whenever he had need, because he thought it would be a sin against such a friendship as theirs to bear alone those cares, which though trifling, are sufficient to spoil most of our pleasures; besides this, Jehuda was too noble-minded to differ in the last from these views, and if he had required it, he would in the same manner have made use of his friend's property. But Alonzo considered it wrong to assume the appearance of a benefactor by the use of another's riches, especially where a liberal man like Abarbanel was ready to tender his support. "But," continued he, in reflection, "if I cannot succor her with riches, I may be useful to her by mental help; I may carefully guard this young plant, and this is a gallant duty, at a time when every step of the Israelite is fraught with danger." Alonzo felt flattered at the idea of becoming the guardian of her virtue, and her protector against all insults; this was a resolution which was worthy of him, and which he felt not only able, but called upon to perform. Absorbed in such thoughts, he was suddenly disturbed by some noise near him. He looked round and percived near him an old Moor, who looked anxiously at him.

"Do not be afraid old man; how is it that the early morn sees you here among these ruins?"

The old man looked at him wildly. "Ruins, ruins, Christians, yon are a fool; it is a fine place; my Edla lives here;

Boabdelin lives here, Mahomet lives here ; Allah lives here— everything lives here among the ruins, Christian." With this words he furiously beat his breast and tore the sleeves of his coat, and Alonzo perceived, with terror, that the man was a maniac.

" Who is Edla?" asked he, with compassion.

" Edla, beautiful Elda?" repeated the old man, approaching him familiary, and then whispering in Alonzo's ear : " They have offered sacrifice to the man upon the large cross, yonder, yonder," said he, pointing to the valley of oranges near Granada.

Alonzo grew pale when the sun shone on the emaciated features of the Arab, whose face was furrowed with deep wrinkles, and his long beard flowed down his shoulders. The old man again opened his lips and gnashed his teeth, repeating several times his former exclamation.

" Are there yet men in Granada with long black robes ? They are devils, Christian, all black devils ; they have sung a Song of Death, Christian." The old man began to imitate, with a horrible voice, a sacred hymn, in a manner which pierced the very soul of Alonzo.

He attempted to leave the place, and unthinkingly gave a handful of small coin to the man, who strewed them on the ground, crying, " I will sow, Christian ; you shall see what beautiful maize will come, for I am hungry."

Alonzo attempted to lead him away, but the old man rushed away with fury and climbing hastily over the rook, careless of the thorns which ran into his naked feet, he dashed into the mountains, crying out, " Edla, daughter Edla," as he disappeared behind the bushes. Alonzo led his horse back to Granada, wrapt in deep thought—thought that now began to spread over his life.

CHAPTER XIV.

Bright were the prospects that now opened upon Spain. The Moorish kingdom had ceased to exist, and from the snow-clad Pyrenees to the blue waves of the Mediterranean, every foot of ground owned the sway of Ferdinand, while the day which was to discover a new earth to men was even now beginning to dawn. The world was rousing itself from the slumber and darkness of the middle ages, and those prospects now beamed upon Spain, which, had she wisely followed them out, would have led her on to glory. There are in truth, times in the history of nations, as well as of individuals, when Fortune showers down her most brilliant gifts, and happy is the nation, or the man that knows how to use them. Wealth, fortune and happiness must have been her lot; but, alas! she knew not her blessings, and the fair vision which might have lit up her country with perpetual sunshine, shone but for a moment and then, like a meteor, sunk back into still greater darkness then before.

The Palace of the Alhambra was now filled with confusion by the preparations for the departure of the royal couple for Castille. Abarbanel was likewise to accompany the king, who was highly pleased with the services of the Privy Councillor, and have commended him before the Court for his prudence and activity in arranging the finances of the newly conquered provinces. Nevertheless, envy and jealousy were aroused in the minds of the courtiers, especially the monks. To see a Jew ruling the financial powers of a great kingdom, and to see him do this with a conscienciousness and disinterestedness rarely found in any functionary in that age, was more than they could endure. Besides this, Abarbanel was no ordinary upstart, concealing the meanness of his soul by outward splendor and haughtiness, but a man who united modesty with profound erudition, and whose penetration, knowledge and experience they were unable to match; a man who was not ashamed of his extraction, but considered his guarantee of nobility higher than that of the proudest grandees of Castille. At Court he was surrounded by envious spies, whom he put to shame by his just and equitable actions; by fanatics, eager to convert him, against whom had defended himself by witty and ingenious replies; by covetous and avaricious persons, whom he satisfied by his complacency and his gold; and finally, by some insolent courtiers, to whose overbearing he opposed a noble and reserved conduct. All this, however, was calculated to embitter the life of a man who loved the quiet pleasures of science and domestic seclusion, and as he cared not for ambition, he would willingly have renounced the brilliancy of his situation, had not his interest for his suffering nation, and his endeavors to protect them against persecution, detained him in the neighborhood of the throne. In this respect he knew the power of his gold, and his influence ; he employed all the means within his reach, and was ready to draw even more intricate snares around the intrigues he had to encounter.

But I feel it is time to tell my reader something of the early life of this man.

Don Isaac Abarbanel was descended from one of the most ancient and celebrated families of Spanish Jews who inhabited Seville. His father emigrated to Portugal and settled in Lisbon, where Don Isaac was born, in the year 1437. Having recived a careful education, and having been in early years initiated into the antiquities of his nation, he was one of those to home, when in the spring of life, science offers charms ever new, surpassing all other pleasures, and forming right objects for the mind to seek. At his period there was kindled within him the first spark to love, a passion that with interior characters has but a feeble and short-lived existence, but gives, generally, men of noble nature an impetus to great and generous deeds. And such was its effects upon Don Isaac, inspiring him with the purest sentiments, without destroying those ambitions which constitute a part of a good mans character. His chief desire was to enrich his State with the wealth and knowledge inherited from his forefathers, and to graft upon the minds oft he peopble those philanthropic lessons taught by the wise men of Israel. Abarbanel became a true friend to Alpheus the Fifth, who made him his Prime Minister. In this capacity he surrounded himself with all that was necesary to strengthen his power and aid him in wielding to his purposes the great masses of men. At no time, however, was he forgetful of his descent, and his constant endeavers to act in accordance with the great examples set before him prevented him from falling into those errors usual to men in his high position.

On the death of the king, and the succession of Don Juan

the Second, came the trying period of his life. Calumny began to do its work, and Don Isaac, accused of treasonable intercourse with the House of Braganza, was obliged to flee to Castille, losing thereby all his property, and, what to him was still more deplorable, all his books and manuscripts.

But he did not remain long in obscurity. His connections and reputation drew him to the palace of Ferdinand and Isabella, where we find him eight years after the last named occurrence.

He transferred hurriedly to his son the duties that devolved on him in Granada, imploring Jehuda to protect those who used to look to him for protection, and not forget the interesting Dinah, whose love for the youth he looked upon wih satisfaction and pleasure.

CHAPTER XV.

The friend at whose house Dinah took up her abode was an old physician, named Arama. He had traveled much in his younger days, and was, therefore, a very situable guardian and companion. In fact, the intimacy was desirable to both parties : for Arama's protection was valuable to Dinah, and Dinah's aid in the education of his two grandchildren was greatly desired by Arama. She therefore, directly followed out her intentions, and changed her residence on the day after Abarbanel left her. But to resume the thread of our story :

When Alonzo returned from the ruins of Illiberis, he had proposed to repair immediately to Dinah's house, when an order from his Colonel summoned him unexpectedly to duty in the palace. Here he passed a painful day and a wearisome night ; and it was not till the following day that he was enabled to gratify his longing desire to visit the abode of Dinah. How surprised was he to hear that on the preceding day on old man had visited her, and that on the very morning of his arrival she had left the house, but whither he was unable to ascertain. He stood on the threshold of the empty room, vacant and stupefied, when something lying on the floor caught his wandering eyes. He picked it up, and finding that it was a piece of paper with some Hebrew written on it, took possession of it, rejoicing that it would give him an opportunity of revisiting Dinah, and immediately set out to seek his friend, whom, however, he did not find at home. Agitated and distressed, he paced and re-paced the streets, forgetting to do what would have appeared most natural, namely, to repair to his own house, where, in fact, Juhuda had been waiting for him some hours. At last they met.

"By heaven, Alonzo, if his Majesty King Ferdinand has slept all the time you have waiting on him, Arragon will be in a very bad state. Here have I been sytting on thorns, waiting for you for more than two hours."

"And if you had sat on thorns all the time while I have been looking for you, you would be in a desperate condition, I assure you." Jehuda smiled and embraced his friend, to whom he then communicated the change which his father himself had had made in the situation of his protege ; of the favorable impression which she had made ipon him (the father), and of his intention of having her soon reside in his own house. The ingeniuosness with which he related this would not have not led any one to suppose that any deep impression had been made upon Jehuda's heart, and in fact his mind was almost too childish to consider the interest that he took in Dinah as real love. Alonzo's heart rejoiced as he listened and argued with the true selfishness of a lover, that he need not expect rivalry from this quarter, at least.

The two youths has now reached Arama's house, and Alonzo recollected the paper which he had found. They accordingly entered and found Dinah engaged in telling an Arabian story to little Joseph. She welcomed them and promised to tell the child the rest of the story in the evening.

"Don't let us interrupt you, dear sister," said Jehuda—it was by this name he had addressed her the day before, and she did not seem to dislike the familiarity—"proceed, I love to hear children's tales, especially from such lips as yours. I remember, even now, with how much pleasure I used to hear the tale which our old duenna told me about the princess Zerura and the three children of the Castle near the Tejo."

But Joseph would not allow any one to listen, and the tale was therefore deferred to the evening. Alonzo delivered the paper into Dinah's hands, for which trifling service she thanked him with a blush. The conversation then turned upon Dinah's present situation, which she described as being exceedingly pleasant. Jehuda then fetched a guitar, that his friend might hear the silvery voice of his new sister, and Dinah sang a song which was loudly applauded by both Jehuda and Alonzo. Dinah then showed them the fine prospect from the balcony; the verdant vineyards which rose in terraces on the deeply wooded mountains of Alpuxares, and it was while they were enjoying the landscape that they were interrupted by the entrance of Arama, covered with dust and weary with exertion. Having been introduced to the young men, he joined in the conversation.

"I have been far in the world, young gentlemen," said he; "I have wandered through the desert to the pyramids of Egypt and to the ruins of Rhamases, which the children of Israel built; for ten days I have traversed the desert, through which Moses led our forefathers for forty years; and for a whole year I went daily to Jerusalem to offer up my prayers in the Holy City; but then I was young, now I am fatigued even by walking through the streets of Granada. It is even according to the old proverb, ' A physician in distress is blind,' which means, 'that if one cannot help himself,' it is difficult to succor others.' "

"Therefore, it would be better to retire and enjoy the fruits of your active life," said Dinah, bringing him some wine and cake, and drawing him to the divan.

"Retire, my daughter!" said Arama; "who would wish to retire, as long as there is marrow in his bones? Were I to do that, I should justly incur the censure contained in the words of ou rsages : 'The best of physicians is doomed to perdition.'"

"A hard sentence, and poor consolation for the disciples of Galen," remarked Jehuda.

"For the bad ones, my dear senor, for the bad; for our sages meant to say, that however scrupulous a physician may be in the fulfillment of his duties, he may easily commit a fault, or perhaps indulging in his own convenience may leave

a pure patient waiting too long. Thus he will surely have
something to answer for, and our duties are indeed great."

"Or, perhaps," continued Jehuda, "he may charge a few
marvedis too many for some bitter herb. I do not wish to
insinuate, my dear Arama......"

"Never mind, senor," replied the physician, as he seated
himself leisurely on the divan and took his glass of wine and
drank it, after having recited the usual blessing. "Never
mind; our sages say again, 'A physician who cures for nothing
is little esteemed.' Believe me, a cheap rule for a young
physician, who wishes to prosper, is 'The dearer the mixture,
the better it is; the cheaper the physician, the sooner he will
be thought a quack.' The physicians sought after are those
who blush if they are *not* paid; not those who blush on receiving
payment. I am an old physician, and have been in Greece,
and there every doctor is attended by his servant carrying a
purse, while the heavier the purse is, the more ready people
are to fill it."

The little ones then climbed on the knees of their grand-
father, who kissed them heartily, gave them some cake, and
then looked with a smile at Dinah, who stood at the corner of
the divan.

Alonzo looked with emotion on the group, and especially
on Dinah, who fixed her eyes on the ground when she met
those' of Alonzo. Jehuda's fingers played with the strings of
the mandolin.

"The boy shall be a physician, senor," said Arama, stroking
Joseph's locks; "in two years he shall begin the Talmud, and
Galen you can get through the whole world."

The two friends were invited to dine and accepted the invi-
tation. Jehuda sat opposite Arama, and Alonzo faced Dinah,
the children occupied the lower end of the table. The leader
of the conversation was the old physician, who indulged in the
pleasure of relating his travels, intermingling his narrative
with Talmudical and Biblical sayings. After dinner the two
children recited their prayers aloud, while the old man did the
same in a suppressed voice, looking at the same time, now on
Dinah and now on Jehuda, as if some idea relating to them were
just striking him. A number of patients, who were waiting in

the ante-chamber then obliged Arama to withdraw; and as the youths could not with propriety prolong their visit, they took their leave, being heartily requested by the old man to repeat their visit as quickly as possible.

CHAPTER XVI.

Jehuda was now to be seen daily in the bazaar, near the Cathedral, buying presents for his sister, and then hastening down the large street, in order to lay them before her and to read in her eyes the triumph of his good taste. It is by these tender attentions to the trifling wants that men of refined feelings charm the minds of others and draw them closer to themselves, not by the strong chain of a great benefit, but by a succession of those nameless offices of kindness which knit heart to heart with a powerful though silken tie. Great benefits excite esteem and admiration; but those feelings are often destroyed by a feeling of submission, which in mean souls, is soon changed to ingratitude; but the little deeds of affection, so important themselves in the souls of men that they soon unite us in love and friendship with aband as it were of flowers. Alonzo could not vie with his friend in his respect; a nosegay of sweet-smelling orange blossoms mingled with fruit, or a wreath of blooming lenticus, were the only gifts which he could bring to his beloved;— and yet she received those with a deeper feeling than the bracelets and guitar of Jehudah; the one she met with merry laugh and loud joy, but the other with a swelling heart, and a secret pleasure which she would not that any should percive. The two friends themselves were much changed by their intercourse with Dinah; they forgot all their other pleasures, even their rambles in the surrounding country; both lived only for her. Jehudah carried the liveliness of his character to the house of Arama and there indulged it to the full, not a little helped by the witty and cheerful conversation of the physician. But Alonzo, on the other hand, changed from cheerful to melancholy; for the light of his life now full upon its true focus— love—rendered him insensible to all else. Nevertheless,

Dinah did not perceive the difference for she had never known
him otherwise; but notwithstanding she felt her heart beat
higher and her pulse throb quicker when in presence of the
Spanish Captain.

One day, urgent business for his father who had left him
guardian of poor during his absence, prevented Jehuda from
paying his customary visit to Arama's house, and Alonzo
accidently went alone. It happened also that the old physician
was absent; so that when he entered he found Dinah standing
by herself at the window, wrapped in thought as she watched
the shadowy figures of the monks entering the Benedictine
Monastery opposite in the dim twilight. He stood gazing at
her with straining eyes, until she suddenly turned and perceived him. She started at the moment, but quickly recovered
her self-possession. Alonzo immediately addressed her :

"So thoughtful, Senora, and alone?" said he, genlty
approching her. She pointed to the Monastery opposite,
which had been lighted up so that the Monks were seen through
the windows. They were seated at a table, and apparently
engaged in serious conversation.

"With all the mischief that those societies have done in the
world," said Alonzo, "I cannot but admire the resolution to
renounce the world, and give up life to holy purposes alone.
Besides the rule of these monasteries at once cuts the tie which
binds us to the earth, and it is well for the distressed that there
is a place were repose may be found."

Dinah shook her head. "I cannot agree with you, Senor ;
for I think it a cowardly retreat from the struggles of life.
And even the sinner should make amends to the world he has
injured."

"But when all our wishes have passed away ; when we have
lost what is dearest to us ; when we are disgusted with the
impulses of ambition ; when disappointed or thwarted, lone
has remained all our taste for pleasure—"

The moon here broke from the clauds above Benedictine
Monastery, and as the gentle rays fell on the pale countenance
of Dinah, he perceived that her eyes were filled with tears.
He took her hand and drew it hastily to his lips; she gently
withdrew it.

"That grief must be a great one, Senor, since you are so young and have already experienced it." She said this in a trembling voice and melancholy tone which pierced him to the heart.

"Dinah," said he, bursting into a passionate exclamation and giving full vent to his excited feelings, "Dinah, no Monastery could cover my grief, no priest could ease it." With these words he drew her towards him, and she yielding to the irresistible impluse of love, leaned her head on his shoulder, and the tears of the Jewess fell on the cross of honor of the Christian Captain.

"Maiden of my soul, your love shall be as the star of my life; Dinah, Dinah, since the evening I first met you, not a minute has elapsed that I have not thought of you. Glory, honor, bravery, all the sentiments which inspired me before, are only the satellites which move around the sun of my love; O! do not banish them Dinah; for if the sun sinks down they will vanish into darkness."

Dinah disengaged herself from his arms. "Don Alonzo, Spanish Captain," she said at length, in a solemn voice, interrupted by sobs, as she turned away her face and covered it with her hands, "you love a Jewess, and the hope of my life is broken ; for duty bars the way, and the cross of belief stands between us."

"Belief, Dinah, belief is happiness ; and then belief is but a fiction. Leave it then, beloved one, for you are mine ; it was first learned to know and understand the beauties of your mind. What are the laws for which men have toiled when compared with love ! They are like tomb-stones on the frame of ruined happiness; they foster not the flowers of pleasure, but leave them to wither and perish. Love is more powerful than the law; for love is life; it is the image of the God-head comprehending all. O! if you wake me from these visions with the cold touch of dull reality, my awaking will be death."

During these words Dinah had turned her face towards him, and stood like one of those splendid sculptures of antiquity wherein the expression of the mind gleams through the dead marble. But within the light of affection shone, on her pale countenance majesty mingled with grace, and a sweet smile

was on her lips as she listened to words such as she had never
before heard, words which carried her soul into the sublime,
and yet brought it nearer to earth. "O! Alonzo," said she as
he finished his passionate outburst; but she could say no more,
her spirits failed her; she covered her face with her hands and
sobbed aloud.

At the same moment a confused noise of several voices was
heard at the door, which was shut with a crash that made the
house tremble, and in the room a picture fell from the wall—
the portrait of Dinah's father. She looked up and rushing
to the place picked up the picture and sank exhausted on the
divan; just then Arama entered, followed by the duenna
with lights.

"Cursed be the land whose ruler is paralyzed," exclaimed
he furiously; "since those cursed Spaniards have been in
Granada all order is at an end." Here he perceived the Spanish
Captain, and seemed embarrassed at his exclamation.

"Our friend, Don Alonzo—pardon the outbreak of my
indignation. The new populace which you have just brought to
the town, and now would drink the blood of Moors and Jews—
this populace compared with our old Arabian rabble, is like
Gemara and Mishna; the former tells us what the latter meant.
Good God! it is now thirty years since I saw the Turks enter
Constantinople; they at least, spared men like me who carry
life with them. I was going to visit an old Moor, a man of
some rank, who always behaved very kind to me. On going
thither I met the servant of a Christian Marquis, who ordered
me to come directly to his master, who was suffering from
fever. I told him to wait till my return from the dying Moor.
The man got furious; a young Spanish doctor offered him his
services, and the people who had meanwhile gattered round,
pursued me to the very door of my house."

The noise before the house gradually ceased. Meanwhile
Arama had quite recovered from his terror. Dinah approached
him, and he attempted to calm her anxiety, but the event of
the preceding hour made her tremble in all her limbs and she
leant pale and almost senseless on his shoulder. Alonzo saw
it with terror and rushed towards her saying "you are unwell,
Senora; help Arama." Arama hastily left the room, but soon

returned with a vial full of scent, which he gave to Alonzo and then hastened away to prepare some medicine for the maiden. Dinah refused Alonzo's support and threw herself on the chair. "Poor Dinah, my daughter," said the old physician on his return, "take this beverage, it will do you good. The furious people! how they spoiled the evening I intended to spend so pleasantly with my Dinah. Don Alonzo, you are a good Christian or a good man; but I assure you that your Spain will have a fate like that of Sodom and Gomorrah. Great God! we are to be good citizens, but they will not leave us any domestic pleasure; we are to love our King, but he treats us like a tyrant; we are to join in brotherly union with you, but you chase us like wild beasts; to sum all, you sour hatred, and expect to reap love."

A knock was heard at the door, and soon afterwards the duenna introduced a Benedictine Monk. As he entered he cast a searching glance on the old physician, and then on Alonzo and Dinah; his lips were thin and colorless, his brow was furrowed, and in his dark and keen eyes was seen an expression of deep cunning.

"Are you the Jewish physician Arama?"

"Yes, worthy father."

"The priest of our Monastery requests you to come to him immediately, as he felt some indisposition during the evening prayer."

"I am ready," said Arama. Another knock was heard, and Jehuda entered greeting his friends with his usual serenity. Arama excused himself for leaving them: "Not even in their repose can the wicked rest," murmured he as he went.

The Monk looked at him as if he understood his words though he spoke in Hebrew. When Arama and the Monk departed, Jehuda asked the reason of the strange agitation perceptible in everything, and Alonzo detailed to him Arama's adventure.

"Arama is foolish," said Jehuda; "he might have gone to the Castilian and felt the pulse of the Moor an hour later." So saying, he sat down by the side of Dinah, asking her a hundred questions while Alonzo was pacing the room. After the lapse of an hour, Arama returned; the priest's indisposition was of little consequence, but he had detained him to question him about his family. It was late when the young men departed, and Alonzo's heart was filled with happiness from the evening he had passed. But Destiny had already set her hand to the wheel of Fortune.

CHAPTER XVII.

On the following evening, the old physician was reciting Psalm CXVIII. while tears rolled down his cheeks on the book, and his eyes were raised to heaven. He was sitting on a silk cushion, leaning his head on his hand, and dressed in his festival garments. A magnificent robe of blue silk was wrapped around him, and on his head glittered a turban set with costly pearls. On the table which was covered with a splendid cloth, stood a silver dish containing unleavened bread and green herbs, a silver cup filled with Malaga, and four candlesticks with waxlights. Dinah was sitting at his side; she had laid aside her mourning dress, for it was the feast of the Passover—of deliverance from the bondage of Egypt—; she was dressed in white satin and on her forehead was a tiara, for Arama wished her to wear it, because on the day of deliverance the children of Israel should deem themselves princes; and on this occasion was it that he had taken from its shrine this ornament as well as a silver girdle for her. Joseph sat on Dinah's knees, as she explained to him the pictures in the book before her. Sarah lay sleeping on a divan.

Celebrating feast of freedom, poor nation—of that freedom which you won on the banks of the Nile. Deem yourselves kings, ye pitiable knaves. Thousands of years rolled down the stream of time, and long ago has the good vanished for which you offer hymns of praise. Do ye not hear the rattling of the chains which are soon to enslave you? Hark! the fire crackles for the sacrifice.

"It is a sublime idea," said Arama; "and to me who have seen the world, a most sublime one to think that on this day all the children of Israel, from the shores of the Euphrates and perhaps even to the shores of India, to the Tejo, are all sitting down to praise *one* God, to celebrate *one* feast and all in the same manner, with the same holy ceremonies."

"But have they all the same pious feelings as you, good father?"

Arama shrugged his shoulders. "Perhaps not all; but many of them have surely more devotion. Alas! the feast of freedom has often been a feast of tears; often have we, in the midst of this festival, been accused of hideous crimes, which the mind of a Jew cannot conceive, much less his hands carry out. On this day of deliverance has death often appeared to our brethern, not in the calmness of home but on the burning pyre, or from the hand of the executioner; often has the way to the land of promise lain through a sea of blood."

He then related to Dinah some of the misfortunes which had befallen his people, when a noise was heard in the antechamber; the door opened and some Spanish soldiers, accompanied by three monks, entered the room. Arama rose to met them with fearful and trembling steps, while Dinah looked on with amazement.

"In the name of the Holy Inquisition," said one of the monks, "follow me Arama." The speaker was the same who had visited them the evening before.

"I pray you, sirs; a mistake—it must be a mistake," said the old man, in a faltering voise; "I am the well-known physician, David Arama, and have practiced my profession here for twenty years, succoring Jews, Christian and Mohamedans without distinction. What can the Holy Inquisition want of me? I am a Jew—a Jew celebrating his Passover—this is my foster-daughter, those are my children: we are all Jews, we are not baptised; we are not Marannos, who have disregarded an assumed religion—you must surely be mistaken."

The monks raised a laugh. "In the name of the Holy Inquisition, do not delay; you will be informed of your crime at some other place; but now you must give over your pagan ceremonies and come with us."

Dinah stepped forward, and in a tone of dignity said, "Worthy father—do not disturb the peace of this pious old man. He is innocent of any crime; his actions are pure as the light, and from early morn to latest night he practices his beneficient occupation."

" We have not to judge of his guilt or innocence, fair lady,"
said one of the monks. " We have only to obey our superiors."

Little Sarah here awoke, and screamed loudly at the sight
of the strange figures, and Joseph clasped the knees of his
grand-father, crying out, "I shall not let you go with these
people ; this is the ugly monk from the Monastery opposite,
who carries away disobedient children."

Dinah threw herself at the feet of the monks. " Take me
prisoner ; let the responsibility fall on me. He is the grand-
father of orphan children. By all that is sacred, I will answer
for him."

Arama now stepped forward with composure, and said,
" Cease, Dinah, and remain here, for the children require your
care ; take them, and preserve the Jewels of my life. I will go.
I fear nothing, for the Lord is with me, and will surely make
his righteousness appear in the midst of my distress ; wait but
for a few moments,. and I will accompany you."

He stepped to the table, recited a blessing, tasted the wine,
broke of the bread and having given some to the children,
turned to the East, and said, "The Lord shall preserve thy
going out and coming in." He then laid his hands upon Dinah
and Sarah, saying : "May the Lord bless and preserve you
and give you peace ;" and finally laying his hand upon Joseph,
he said, " The angel who redeemed me from all will bless
the lad."

While these things were passing the monks stood perfectly
still waiting for Arama, who when he had finished, kissed the
parchment on the door-post, and without looking back, passed
from the house, leaving Dinah praying in tears.

CHARTER XVIII.

It was a terrible night for Dinah—even more terrible than
that on which her father died. He had departed into the
region of peace ; he had left the earth in freedom ; there she
stood alone in the world, but the charity of her nation led her
to expect some succor and relief. But this day had taken her
second father from her, and led him to a mysterious tribunal,

from which but few returned. And he had been snatched away, too, from the midst of a peaceful feast, from the arms of his lovely grand-children, whose fate pressed heavily upon her. And her own heart, how changed it was! The strength of her father's belief had been shaken in her mind by the insinuation of a man belonging to a race which showered all these misfortunes upon her people, and the powerful agency of first love ruffled the stream of her life, 'ere now flowing on gently and smoothly, touched only by the breezes of domestic peace. And yet it was the picture of that man which brightened the terrified soul of Dinah, with the sacred hope of safety and from whom she expected counsel and the deliverance of Arama. She stepped on the balcony and looked through the darkness upon the streets, whose stillness was interrupted only by the dashing of the waves of the Darra, and by the watch, the words of the sentinels. Opposite stood the Monastery, dark and gloomy as the grave. Just then the morning began to dawn, and the sun rose in brightness over the summit of the Aluxares, casting his rays upon the countenance of Dinah.

But when the bustle became more and more lively, when she still remained alone, and the duenna whom she had sent returned without any intelligence of her father, when the patients waiting in the ante-chamber were dismissed, and the children awoke sobbing for their grandfather, a knock was heard at the door. Jehuda entered, pale and disordered. "Where is Arama, Dinah?" was his first question. Dinah told him with tears, what had happened, implored him for immediate assistance, and solicited him to use all his efforts to save the brave Arama. Jehuda stood stupefied; his eyes rolled wildly and his face glowed with such passion as he had never known before. "Something fearful is about to happen," said he; "Arama was carried off last evening, and Alonzo taken also by the officers of justice. Revenge upon those hated monks!"

Dinah screamed, and wringing her hands madly, cried, "Alonzo, my Alonzo, have you then perished!"

Jehuda started, and catching Dinah as she was falling to the ground laid her on a chair, and, looking up to heaven said, "Thy Alonzo?—Thou hastvanished, a star of my hope! But I may not stop; I will go on with what I have begun. Already am I a man." His mind saw it all now, and he smiled bitterly, as he gazed upon the maiden. At this moment the Monk entered, accompanied by soldiers, and demanded the keys of the receptacle in which Arama's jewels were deposited. Jehuda would have given way to his feelings of revenge had not caution mastered him. But, when the Monk remained deaf to all the entreaties and inquiries of Dinah; when he looked round the room with a malignant look and insisted on his demand, Jehuda approached him : " Who art thou, Monk, and who has sent thee here ?"

"Who I am," said the Monk, "*these* (pointing to the soldiers) will tell you. Beware of insulting the servant of the Church, unless you would draw down on you the flashes of the tempest which stand over your head, Jew ! We know you, Jehuda Abarbanel, and your proud race who, relying on their riches, would think to sell the Church; but beware !" The soldiers drew around the Monk; Dinah gave him the keys, and having emptied the box, they left the house.

CHAPTER XIX.

Near the glittering serpentine quarries of Granada stood an old edifice. The Moors, in the time of their glory, had erected there an hospital in which they offered a refuge to homeless pilgrims and old men, who had lost every relation, and in which Imans were appointed to read the Koran from morning till night. Since the victory of the Spaniards nobody knew what use was made of this building; the poor and the priests had been driven out and numerous sentinels surrounded and guarded the entrance. The Moors imagined that the treasures of the Alhambra were deposited there, because in the Alhambra itself the ghosts of their kings terrified the Christians. It was well known that beneath that edifice there were vast subterranean passages which led to the quarries. In these vaults those who had died in the hospital had been buried, and he who descended into them left the warm atmosphere of the orange-grove for the chill charnel-breath of the tomb. The passages were now parted in small divisions, made by iron bars, and chains had been attached to the walls, to which prisoners were bound.

It was midnight. The iron doors opened ; some lay-brothers appeared with torches, and led up the old man, whose eyes were dazzled by the sudden rays of light that streamed upon him, and who followed his guides with staggering steps. His grey hair was damp and disorderly ; upon his countenance were tears ; shudders of cold and fear made his limbs tremble ; and with this sight strangely contrasted the festival and oriental garment which the dirty prison had soiled. It was Arama, the Jewish physician. He was led over several staircases till his knees faltered, and his companions indignantly refused to let him lean on them, and seemed to fear his touch as infectious. They arrived in a spacious hall lit by torches ; round a large table sat several men in the habits of Franciscan monks ; at one end of the table sat the master of the assembly, his eyes fixed upon some papers, from which he raised them slightly on the entrance of the prisoner, but soon resumed his former attitude. In the hall were the images of the apostles and saints ; a large image of the holy virgin was opposite the entrance ; in the walls were many shrines, all filled with papers, and on the table stood a large crucifix made of gilt wood.

For half an hour the prisoner stood among his guides ; not the least noise interrupted the dreadful silence, only Arama whispered gently so that none could hear it, "Blessed art thou, O Lord, that thou hast made me an Israelite." Suddenly the Inquisitor turned to him, asking him his name and age. Arama prepared himself to reply, and an almost youthful fire seemed to animate the limbs of the old man.

"My name is Rabbi David Arama, son of Rabbi Abraham Arama, son of Joseph, son of David, son of Obadja Arama, from Fez. The days of the years of my pilgrimage on earth are seventy ; few and evil have the days of the years of my life been, and have not attained unto the days of the years of my fathers in the time of their pilgrimage."

When questioned about the earlier part of his life he answered, " I was twelve years of age when I was bereft of my father. I was then brought up by the venerable, now deceased, Rabbi Michael Sacuth, who instructed me in the faith of our forefathers and in doctrines of our sages. The science of medicine I learned from Abenhamed, an honored physician in

Malaga. At the age of twenty I set out on my travels, during
which I have seen many countries and nations. I traversed
France and Italy, embarked at Trani and sailed to Greece;
I journeyed through Syria and the Promised Land of my
ancestors; I offered up my prayers on the ruins of the Temple,
and have seen the City of the Lord, once a queen among the
provinces, but now solitary and desolate; I visited the ruins
of Babylon and mourned under the willows upon which our
ancestors hung their harps; I saw the opulent Bagdad; my
soles burned with the sands of the desert, when I visited the
tomb of Ezekiel, and amid thousands of my people erected the
tabernacles in the desert, and celebrated the memory of the
glorious days of my ancestors. Even the remote Lusa, where
the grave of Daniel may be seen, was not too distant for me.
I then turned back from the cities of the East to the West. I
then came to Byzantium, the City of the Seven Hills, just at
the time when the proud Moslem dethroned the Greek emperor,
and entered the ungrateful daughter of Rome with furious
hosts to unfurl the standard of his prophet on the top of Aja
Sophia. I saw the heads of the Greeks tramped upon by the
hoofs of the Arabian steeds, and with a shudder I recall the
calamities which befel the Christians in the East. Thence I went
to Egypt, the mother-land of my profession, where the royal
Pharaohs lie cold in their mighty catacombs. The thirst for
knowledge also induced me to visit those empires which the
sons of Ishmael have established in the North, and I travelled
to Fez, the birth-place of my ancestors. After thirteen years
wandering I returned to Granada, where I have practiced for
thirty-eight years the art of a physician. Worthy fathers! no
vice has ever stained the course of my life ; every day brought
its own labors, troubles and cares. I have seen my wife and
children buried, and in honor attained the term of a man's life,
and any further extent of life will be the peculiar favor of God."

These words, though spoken with great emotion, had no
effect upon the assembled judges, who, like potentates of
darkness, fixed their staring looks upon him.

"David Arama," said the Inquisitor, in a penetrating
tone, "you stand before the holy Inquisition, whose province
it is to bring to light the crimes committed against the

Christian faith and the Catholic Church. Speak the truth in answer to the question I am going to put to you, or else your punishment will be doubled and you will be delivered up to everlasting perdition through the revengeful hands of your worldly judges. Who is the maiden that lives in your house under the title of your daughter?"

Arama spoke the truth: he told them of Dinah's origin; who had entrusted her to his care, and how she promised to be the prop of his old age.

The Franciscan monk then arose from his seat, advanced quickly towards the old man, and said with a dreadful voice:—

"David Arama, you stand accused of having by persuasion and menaces, prevented that maiden from joining the Christian faith and from entering as was her intention, within the pale of the only true Church, laying aside the errors of your cursed heresy; you stand accused of having described to her the Christian religion as an abomination, and tormented her mind by criminal conversation. You have snatched from her hand the book of the Evangelist, and burnt upon your hearth the image of the crucified. What have you to say in answer to these accusations?"

Arama stood calm and composed; he looked around among the circle of the monks, stepped a few paces forward and said:—

" Worthy fathers, these reproaches with which you attack me are perfectly novel to me. He who has seen the world as I have would never dishoner a belief differing from his own ; even if he were possessed of such a degree of self will, policy would induce him to suppress it. Dinah is a faithful Jewess; she never entertained even the most distant idea of rejecting that creed which her father's precepts have engraved upon her heart. Never—I swear it by the God of heaven and earth, by Him who has been, is and be,—by the Almighty Zebaoth !— never did she give me occasion to throw aspersions on the Christian faith, never did she show a desire of turning to you, and never have I insulted your Saints as you accuse me. Far be it from me to do such a thing and thus to show a contempt for the religion of those whom I have so often saved from the hand of death, whose last sighs I have heard, whose agonies I have endeavored to ease, whose death-hour

I have honored, and to whom I have often myself sent their priest. Inquire about Arama in Granada; who is the man that can accuse me of this? who has seen me commit such actions? Respected fathers you have only wanted to try me; you have carried me away from my dear grandchildren, from the celebration of the Passover, and from patients who anxiously long for my assistance—you will give me justice, for you are the ministers of your faith as I am of mine. But the God who appeared to Abraham, whom Jacob saw in his vision—you fear Him as I do; the pure flame of his love penetrates your heart as it does mine; you cannot, you will not leave the man of seventy years to languish in this subterranean dungeon. From this depth I call to the Lord—you call yourselves his priests; be then the messengers of his mercy, the harbingers of his love; restore me to my children; let me celebrate this festival in the light of day and I will praise you amidst the people."

Arama seemed exhausted; he looked at the monks with tearful eyes; his breath was quickened and agitated, and the agony of suspense was depicted in his countenance.

"You wish to know your accuser," answered the Inquisitor; "your accuser is a Christian who has visited your house and who has seen with his own eyes the wretched situation of the maiden, and to whom she confided her desire for baptism, and the restraint under which you hold her—it is the royal Captain—Ferdinand Alonzo."

Arama was thunderstruck. "Ferdinand Alonzo!" he stammered; "where am I? O! now it is all clear to my mind. Worthy fathers, the Captain has deceived you and me. O! shame upon the time when youth belies old age. What does Alonzo want of me? I hospitably recieved him in my house. Is it possible that in the course of conversation an expression fell from my lips which I would not have said before others. But the accusations he throws out against me are unfounded and false—falser than the serpent of Paradise. Alonzo! your eye was so pure and true, your look so noble, your manners so captivating—has passion destroyed your mind and seared your heart even so far that you wish to destroy your aged friend? My tongue is powerless to speak, my eyes contain no more tears by which I could hope to move; lead Alonzo hither, let me see him and he will soon acknowledge his error."

"Do you think, false liar, of shaking the youth in his statements by your dissimulating arts? Know then your hatred against Christianity, your wickedness is proved also from another source. You have refused to succor a suffering Christian and rendered your assistance to a Moorish heretic. When you were called away to the prior, you uttered abusive language; here is the witness."

The Inquisitor touched a bell, which echoed through the vast passage, and in a few moments there entered Gonzago Campanton, called Father Hieronymus of Seville, the Benedictine monk already known to the reader.

Arama staggered backwards. The Inquisitor made a sign to two monks, who rose from their seats, and placed themselves before the Jew, the one with a crucifix, the other with the breviary; between the two stood another monk who read the accusation, while Arama exclaimed repeatedly, "No, no." Gonzago touched the crucifix and confirmed by an oath the truth of his statement, that he came to fetch Arama for the prior, he heard him call the Christian in Hebrew, rebellious and wicked.

The statement of Alonzo was read by two other monks, in the name of the tribunal before whom he was said to have laid it down the preceding day. Another sign from the Inquisitor, and three lay brothers entered with the instruments of torture which were arranged before Arama. The Inquisitor called again upon him to make a confession, or by assuming Christianity to procure his liberty.

"The belief of my fathers I cannot deny; I have grown old in it; my grey head could not understand a new doctrine; should I by a false confession draw down on myself the vengeance of the Most High—should I, as a miserable Maranno, belie the Deity in this assembly? No, Arama is not wicked, he is not a blasphemer, he loves Jews, Christians and Moors, but he will remain true to his God, as he has remained true to mankind."

The rack was prepared. "Thou who giveth strength to the feeble," prayed the old man, "who raiseth the fallen, delivereth those that are bound, send help from Thy sanctuary and do not abandon me in this hour of trouble."

He was then stretched upon the rack; the fingers that hitherto had only felt the pulses of the suffering were tortured with thumb-screws; his groans, his exclamations of "God have mercy on me," echoed from the walls, and some convulsive motions seemed to indicate the approach of death.

The Inquisitor made a sign and Arama was released. They raised him up, he fell backwards into their arms, while his lips uttered the words, "Blessed art thou, O Lord, that thou hast not made me a slave." He was then led away and fell powerless upon his couch of straw. The day broke, but no ray of light fell into his dark prison. From the distance the strokes of Moorish slaves in the quarries were heard.

The sky of Spain is blue and pure, and through her fertile groves nature smiles as fair a smile as that with which she greeted the creation, but even in this earthly paradise has men spread destruction far around, and though the gracious providence of God pours blessings without number on the land, yet man's heart is hardened with guilt, and he listens not to the voice of his Creator.

CHAPTER XX.

Gonzago Campanton, the Benedictine monk, was born at Seville in the year 1444, of Jewish parents. His father had been once a wealthy and respected man, but having lost the greater part of his fortune by several disasters, was obliged to earn his living as beadle to the synagogue, taking the office very reluctantly. He looked with envy upon the wealthy of the community, of whom in better days he had been one, and treated with harshness the poor to whom he had to distribute the charity of the synagogue. Thus he rendered himself disliked by all, and there were frequent complaints and reproofs about his conduct, which contributed still more to embitter his life and to render him still more cruel to his virtuous wife. Woe to the man who is reduced to poverty without greatness being possessed of a certain degree of knowledge and of soul. Indigence then breeds a greater evil—wickedness. The disposition and situation of the father could not fail to produce an influence upon the education of Gonzago, the only son. His father's pride kept him apart from his young co-religionists. With the poor he did not allow him to associate, and the rich would not admit him into their society. Thus he grew up without a youthful friend—without those pleasures of child-hood in which youth should develop and whose sweet recollec-tions refresh us even in manhood and old age. At home his father continually rebuked him for not attending sufficiently to his studies, for Campanton's sole hope rested in this son. Unable to leave him any riches, he wished to make him a miracle of erudition, that the rays of his son's glory might one day fall brilliantly upon his own days. His imagination frequently recurred to the time when he should oppose to the wealth of the rich the fame of his son, highly esteemed by Christians, Jews, and Moors. The son's capacity seemed to justify his high expec-tations; but being goaded by the father's ambition he exceeded the just limits, and thus it happened that the treasures of knowledge were for him rather the morbid food of passion than the beneficial flame of the youthful mind, nourished by the sacred oil of wisdom. Gonzago learned a good deal; in his fourteenth year he not only understood but knew by heart the sacred volume as well as the Talmud; but their doctrines lay heaped up in his memory only, and did not penetrate to the chambers of the heart. He was well versed in astronomical and mathematical science, which was then pursued with greater ardor by the Portuguese and Spaniards, as the means of discover-ing new worlds; but the brightness of the constellations struck only his eye and did not enlighten his soul, or elicit the sparks of feeling which are elevated above the earth and its frailties. He knew the languages of the Greeks, Romans and Arabs, but the greatness of antiquity, and the calmness which pervades the works of the ancients, exercised no influence upon his character. Under such circumstances it is not surprising that he became disgusted with knowledge, and that when in the flower of his age passions began to work upon him, to which he had no adequate force to oppose. He had just terminated his eighteenth year, when he returned from Cordova, where he had pursued his studies. He saw the daughter of a rich Jew, Estrella Benbenaste, and he loved her with all the ardor of his passionate disposition. With impatience he awaited the time when the highest Rabbinical dignities should be conferred upon him; for these he hoped would counterbalance Benbenaste's gold, when he should sue for the hand of his daughter. The moment arrived—he recived those dignities from several academics. Campanto looked triumphantly upon the wealthy of the community, whose sons lost fortune and honor in worldly pursuits—but his insolence increased when he perceived that his son's reputation could not remove the obscurity of his situation. Estrella's hand was refused to Gonzago, not on account of his poverty—for the honor of being related to a great Rabbi fully made up for any sacrifice of money—but from a dislike to the well-known cunning of the father. Besides, Gonzago himself, in spite of his profound erudition, did not possess anyone's confidence, because he lacked those gentle qualities of the heart which can alone captivate the multitude. Then it was that the flame of his passion burst out violently; he cursed the hour of his birth; he hated his nation; he insulted his father, and would at once have abandoned him if he had not been restrained by his mother, who had yet some influence upon the boisterous temper of her son. But at last his father was compelled, by continued complaints, to lay down his office; he entered again into some small business, but his advanced age had diminished his activity, and the family saw themselves reduced to penury. At that time Gonzago learned that a near relative of his mother, named Gaon, had acquired great riches; he lived at Vittoria, and had for some time farmed the tolls of the crown. Gonzago repaired to him to ask advancement for himself and succur for his impoverished father and his poor mother, who in her misery had been struck with blindness. But Gaon was ashamed of his poor relations. He dismissed Gonzago with harsh words, and would not know the family.

Gonzago then wandered about the opulent town, where, in the midst of busy life he was alone, abandoned, insulted and repudiated. Life, stripped of every charm, became to him a burden. Insulted ambition, and rejected love, became the furies which called forth within him the spirit of despair and revenge. He was standing upon a bridge ready to throw himself into the floods, when he suddenly heard a tumult in the neighboring market place. A monk was there exciting the people against the Jews; he described to them their wicked actions, and called upon them to revenge themselves upon the murderers of their Saviour, and the oppressors of Spain, among whom he mentioned Gaon. At this name Gonzago rushed towards the monk, seized the crucifix, and describing the cruel treatment he had received from Gaon, assumed the faith of the Christians and received baptism amid the loud acclamations of the populace. The monk greeted him as a brother, the people thronged to the house of the hated toll-keeper, and the corpse of the unfortunate Gaon was soon thrown from the windows of his house into the street, where the people rudely insulted it, and paraded the head on a pole. The king, though wishing to punish the murderers, and to have the houses of the ringleaders pulled down, was advised to act leniently, and Gonzago was sheltered from persecution by the all-powerful arm of the church.

Forgetting his father and mother, he traversed the country with Franciscan monks, preached against the Jews, and with a diabolical pleasure saw their blood shed and their Rabbis conducted to the funeral pile. But even in this new occupation he waited in vain for honors and dignities, and was often mortified in the midst of his harangues by the mockeries of the people at his Jewish dialect. The enthusiasm which he pretended to possess for his new creed was but coldly responded to, and he often became the butt of the witty monks; and it was only when they attacked the Marannos that they chose him as their leader, because as he was acquainted with all the outward signs of the Mosaic creed, he could best discover the heretics. Thus he became the terror and scourge of the new Christians, who having been forced to assume christianity secretly performed the ceremonies of their former faith; for he surprised them when celebrating the Sabbath or some other festival—when praying in their chambers or instructing their sons. But he himself sank more and more into the mire of sensuality, which consumes alike the powers of body and mind.

At last the government put a stop to this spiritual bully, by compelling him to enter a monastery. Here he spent his days under the rigorous vigilance of a virtuous abbot, whose life he embittered for several years through his intrigues, until he was sent to Granada, and there employed by the Inquisition as an instrument of their outrages. The prior of the Benedictine monastery, an indolent man and brutal voluptuary, employed him as an agent to serve his lusts. The prior had noticed the charming Jewess in Arama's house ; he observed her daily, and he would not have spared any sacrifice to get her into his power. Gonzago was there very useful as a spy, and besides, any office that might supply another victim to his revenge was welcome to him.

The reader is already informed how he fetched Arama to come to the prior ; we know also how he understood those Hebrew words which Arama uttered. Those words were deemed sufficient to found on them an indictment before the Inquisition ; and as they had noticed Alonzo's visits to Arama's house, they guessed their object, and endeavored to throw upon Alonzo also the suspicion of heresy. The unfortunate Arama was taken away from the celebration of his festival and dragged to the prison, where he had to wait several days before he was arraigned at the tribunal ; and on the same night they had also secured the person of Alonzo, from whom they had cunningly elicited the confession of his love for Arama's foster-daughter. He thought he could not commit any crime by telling them the manner in which he was first introduced to Dinah, for whom, in fact, he feared more than for himself. But the crafty monks construed all this into an accusation of Arama, which apparently came from Alonzo. Thus the prior and Gonzago had removed from Dinah her father and her lover, and the only one that yet stood in their way was Jehuda, the son of the mighty Abarbanel. But secret information had already reached them of the cruel measures that were planned against all the Jews of Spain, and thus the voluptuous priest hoped the satisfaction of his lusts from the despair of the Jewess. Alonzo's prison was not so dreadful as that of Arama ; but a gloomy melancholy reigned within him, for the thought of the fate of his beloved did not leave him for a moment, and it was in vain that he inquired of his keepers after her or Arama, or for the cause of his imprisonment.

CHAPTER XXI.

In the Court of Ferdinand and Isabella at Madrid, the festivities for the victory over the Moors had not yet ceased. They were, indeed, not those pompous fetes in which, as in the times of chivalry, exploits of bravery formed the prominent feature; nor were they festivals of modern times, where art winds the wreath of enjoyment around the social circle. Then it was an epoch which looked at once to the past and to the future, and the year 1492 may be well termed the close of the Middle Ages. The coloring of the former times had vanished from the customs of mankind, but they had not yet received the decided character which they derived from the discovery of a new world, and from the Reformation. Besides, the Spanish character does not suit loud expressions of joy, which break forth very rarely, and then mostly on religious feasts. Public processions and solemn worship in the churches were the diversions and occupations in which the monkish court of Ferdinand and Isabella indulged. Such spectacles seemed best calculated to express their gratitude to God for the victory of Christianity over Islamism, and at the same time pass away most suitably their leisure.

But that victory was not as yet complete; there yet lived the most ancient and most obstinate enemies to the faith—the Jews; they yet lifted up their heads, though oppressed and persecuted. As long as they were not destroyed the task of making Spain the Catholic kingdom of Europe was but half done. Though they were connected by the ties of relationship with some of the greatest families (who did not refuse to intermarry with the wealthy Jews), what was that to the monks, who were attached only to the see of Rome, and knew no other love but that of power. Though they were the most industrious and active inhabitants of that fruitful land, so much the more were they objects of hatred to the priests, who sought to grasp their possessions. That time had now arrived. Torquemada undertook to persuade the king, who was of a covetous disposition, through the prospect of the immense treasures which he would gain by the expulsion of the Jews from the whole of Spain; and the conscience of the queen was intimidated by her confessor, Ximenes, and the priest, Talavera, who encouraged her to complete the triumph of Christi-

anity by the removal of the Jews—representing to her that the
last victory over the Moors had been a hint from above to retain
religion in its purity, and described the crimes which the Jews
committed by producing old documents, in which they were
accused of having insulted sacred images, murdered Christian
children, and treated the cross with contempt.

Don Abarbanel knew nothing of all this ; such machinations
were concealed even from the Spanish grandees, and how should
they have been known to the Jews? On the contrary, everything
around him wore a smiling appearance. Talavera daily conversed
with him about the sacred writings and doctrines; Ximenes
asked him frequently for the interpretation of some passage or
other. They commanded his zeal in the king's service ; flattered
him with prospects of reward for himself and family, and
anticipated all his desires with the greatest attention imaginable.
This cheered his mind. He saw, in imagination the days when,
the hearts of thousands of the oppressed would be relieved, and
when the splendor of the Moors would be renewed under the reign
of Catholic princes. Thus he replied to their friendliness with
numerous favors, and deemed no sacrifice too great to be offered up
on the altar of friendship.

But suddenly things assumed a different aspect. The priests
began to hold frequent interviews with the rulers. Abarbanel was
frequently refused an audience, though his business was urgent
and important. Short and concise were the answers given him
by the courtiers. He felt the sultriness of the atmosphere around
him, but he could not yet see the coming tempest. He spent the
evenings thoughtfully in his own room, his eyes fixed on the
blue waves of the Manzanaras, or wandering over the country
decked with the bloom of spring. Abarbanel moved now in a
world of ideas: he reviewed his past eventful life, and gloomy
presentiments, which he could not repress, flitted through his
soul. Thus he sat one evening, when suddenly a knock was heard
at the door, and a minute after entered Hidalgo Francisco Corduero. His elevated forehead, his bright black eyes, over-
shadowed by bushy eyebrows, the smile on his lips and the
nobility of his carrrige would have led any one to discover at once
in him a man of high attainments, even if this had not been
so strongly marked in his sonorous voice and the charming har-

mony with which he spoke his native tongue in the Castilian dialect.

"You will pardon my intrusion, Senor; I am rejoiced to find you alone, and—a rare occurrence—unoccupied."

Abarbanel met him with marks of friendship; he now took his hand and led him to the window; "I am occupied, though not with books, yet with thought. But who could be more welcome to me than you?"

Corduero looked at him with a penetrating eye. "I do not think that I am deceived," he observed.

"May I ask in what respect?"

"Abarbanel, you are my friend and I am yours; still more, I am attached to you by the ties of gratitude. For your intercession I am indebted for the preservation of my estates, which the miserable priests were eager to seize. Are you not aware of what is going on in the king's cabinet respecting your co-religionists?"

Abarbanel looked at him with surprise. At the same time his manner betrayed the terror which this question caused him. "For five days I have not visited the court. I was refused an audience from the monarch on account of urgent occupations. I am not accustomed to intrude myself upon my royal patrons. But I am utterly unaware of anything going on there concerning the Israelites, either for good or evil. My word may suffice to assure you of this."

"Then I am not deceived. Abarbanel, you are slumbering on a precipice down which you and all your people are doomed to be thrust. The expulsion and extirpation of the Jews from Spain is being canvassed in the king's council, and perhaps is already decided. An indiscreet page of the queen, who caught up the words of her confessor, made the communication in confidence to my son, who is his friend."

"The talk of a boy, noble Hidalgo," observed Abarbanel; but to support himself he was forced to lean on his sword.

"Would to God it were so, my noble friend; but he was acquainted with too many details about the affair which could not possibly have been his invention. He knew how the queen would not at first consent to the proposal; how they then lessened your merits, Abarbanel; how they spoke of the faults and levity on your son at Granada, and many calumnies that might be

expected from the craft of these hypocritical priests, who have
but to take the criminal thoughts of their own hearts to disfigure
with them the character of any honest man. O, Abarbanel!
these priests will render my poor country the desert of Europe.
Our glory will be the gate to disgrace; the struggle for freedom
of religion will be the first of slavish subjection. They have
begun the work by degrading the nobility; they continue it by
the expulsion of a race, and they will end by the subjection of the
hidalgos and the citizens."

"They cannot wish to do that, Senor, they cannot."

"Don Abarbanel, it is only the free and noble man who cannot
do everything; the villain can do all. You are a man of experience,
my friend, and you remember how you have been treated at the
Court of Portugal. Yet it is time : leave this country; flee, save
your life, for you will be received everywhere with open arms."

"When I fled before Don John," replied Abarbanel, calmly,
inclining his head upon his breast, "it was my person, and that
only, which was persecuted. Now the persecution falls upon the
whole of my people, and I shall not separate my lot from theirs.
Ferdinand will hear me; he heard me when I brought the doub-
loons to carry to the Moorish war. When I tendered succor
against the Islamites, I suppressed my feelings as a Jew to be the
servant of my king—now I will deny the statesman to be a Jew."

"Your resolution is noble, and well worthy of my friend
Abarbanel; but you have children, your dearest son is far from
you, you will draw them into ruin. For who would refuse in
this universal shipwreck to save himself and his own from a
watery grave?"

"The Spanish Jew, Hidalgo, would prefer to be destroyed with
his brethren."

"But you will lose all, even those means by which you might
relieve the distress of thousands of the persecuted."

"Lose all, Hidalgo! What do you call all? Do you mean my
riches? for that is what you name the Jew's all. For surely,"
said he, as he looked through the window upon the country, faintly
illuminated by the rays of the parting sun, "the smiling country
is not his—the blooming Spring, the pure air are not his. Nor are
they yours, Hidalgo; for you stain the earth with human blood,
you infect the air with the curses of the slaughtered, and the Spring

returns only to find your old vices. It renews your spirits, but does not regenerate your mind, hardened more than ever in sinfulness. If I lose what you call my all, I shall gain perhaps what I call my all. I shall accompany my brethren into misery, and be to them an example of manly endurance. God will strengthen me, and give me power to empty with them the cup of poison which your monarch and priests present to us in the name of *Christian* love."

Corduero looked sadly and silently at him.

"You are angry," continued Abarbanel, "on account of my reproachful words; but they are not intended for my friend, who has just given me such a proof of his fidelity. I thank you for your kindness, and I shall make use of it."

After a long consultation the friends parted. Abarbanel worked the whole of the night. Hew rote to Granada to call at once his son to Madrid; hegave warning to the chief Spanish communities, begging of them to be on their guard, and to sell, as soon as possible, their estates; and he prescribed for them measures they should take, if the disaster should happen. He then examined a quantity of old papers relative to the history of the Spanish Jews with the greatest calmness; he turned over those large folios as if he were engaged in some pleasant study, and when he felt fatigued he stepped to the window to inhale the balmy air and to address an ardent prayer to the God of his fathers, and then resumed his work.

The Duke of Sidonia and the priest Ximenes were now announced to him. He received them at the door of the ante-chamber with due reverence, and led them into his room.

"Their majesties, our most gracious monarchs," began Ximenes, "send you greeting, Don Isaac. Their wisdom was pleased to publish an edict relative to your co-religionists, with the contents of which we are commissioned to acquaint you. The disasters which the new Christians have brought over Spain and the ancient Jews, and the embarrassments in which the State has been placed through the numereous emigration of the Marannos, have induced the monarchs to put a stop at once to these unfortunate events and to order all the Jews out of the country, and thus not to expose them to any further persecutions. Our most gracious monarchs have allowed all their Jewish subjects the term of three months to prepare themselves for their journey and to sell their landed property. The edict, which has to-day been published in the two kingdoms, will furnish you with the details of the decree. Don Abarbanel, the king send, you through us, tne assurance of his perpetual favor ; you are excluded from this expulsion, and will enjoy the royal protection—but one thing is demanded of you, and that is, not to interfere with the above affair, and to give up all connection with the Marannos."

Abarbanel looked for some time silently at the two messengers.

"Shall I be allowed to lay my homage at the throne of the monarch ?" he at last asked, in a tone which seemed to indicate that the grace shown him filled him with joy. Ximenes did not know how to reply to this question.

"You shall have an audience," observed the duke, "I can answer for it ; I shall go to the king ; you shall have one even this day." The duke then left him.

"You accept, then," asked Ximenes, "the condition of the royal grace ?"

"I must first personally bring my thanks before the monarch, and learn the contents of the edict."

Ximenes also departed. Abarbanel then perused the edict. He lifted up his eyes to heaven and said, "Thou hast given, thou hast taken away, O Lord, blessed be thy name."

CHAPTER XXII.

In the dark dungeon lay Arama on a bed of straw. The venerable form of the man could no longer be recognized ; the radiance of the eye was gone, the features sunken, and occasionally a low moaning sound—the psalms of fear and repentance—issued from the lips of the wretched man, of no long duration, however, from his extreme prostration. He awaited death; his tremtling right hand grasped the left, as if with wonted skill to guage the remnant of life's tide. The old physician while getting weaker, felt his heart tremble and shuddered at the cold perspiration on his brow ; he longed for a refreshing draught. But where for him was the consoler and helper he to others had so often been ? At last he sank back exhausted; consciousness left him, or happy dreams now played through his deep sleep. Dreams ! for presently he seemed to stand on the ruins of the temple of Jerusalem and heard the lament of the Deity,—"Oh, why did I destroy my house and drive away my childern ?" Or he prayed at the tomb of the kings and an angel's form appeared to him and said,— "Thou must not pray on these ruins, Israelite, thou must not bewail." Dreams ! and he stood in a desert, his eye sought a green spot, he listened for the murmur of waters but in vain. Now appears a man with a radiant face; he strikes a rock with his staff and water of the purest crystal flows ; the fainting man drags himself thither, but at the same instant a monk with contorted face stands beside, keeps him back, and dashes his gray head against the rock; but the thunder rolls and the man with the staff carries him up to the rifted clouds. He awakes and again the monk stands with a light, shaking the old man and ordered him to follow. In vain Arama stretches his aching limbs, but he is forcibly borne away and brought before his judges. Again they stand in the old walls and again appears the crucifix on the table. But Alonzo is there also surrounded by men ; and when his eyes fell on the old man whom they have brought, his cry of terror echoes through the wide halls ; the old man glances at him passing his hand across his brow as if to help him to recall some picture of memory.

"Arama," said the Inquisitor, "here stands your accuser, Don Fernando Alonzo. Doest thou still deny to this face thy crimes ?" At these words Alonzo, enraged, exclaims, "Murderers, I see your plan; I am in no wise the accuser, who brought hither this unfortunate man. *I*, your accuser, Arama ? Do not believe these wretches."

"Silence, infidel," cried the Inquisitor, "else your fate will be like that of the Jew."

"Be my fate a thousand times worse, Monks, my life shall never be stained by treachery."

The Inquisitor raised his thundering voice : "Christian, wilt thou recall thy statement of having had improper intimacy with a miserable Jewess? Or wilt thou deny thy crimes? So shall the chief atone in the deepest dungeons, and the Jew and his daughter ascend the funeral pyre."

These words did not fail to have their effect. Alonzo kept silent; he shuddered; the Monk had touched a sensitive spot in his heart. Aráma looked up timidly; "Miserable fathers," said he, "I am prepared for death; what you said is true; I have hated you all my life indeed and cursed you even in my prison. True also that your God is not mine: he is not love, not charity, for (here he laughed wildly) he rejoices in the death of the sinner. I am an old grey Jew; I sinned even in my mothers womb, miserable fathers, I have sinned all my life, for (here he screamed with all his might) I prayed that upon your heads might fall all the curses of heaven! Punish me, miserable fathers! I deserve it, but let not your anger reach the girl; she is a noble treasure entrusted to me; neither the lad there, for he is a good Christian. Now be quick, or else death will come itself; I am an old physician and have often sharply looked him in the face."

His strength was leaving him; he fell back; he tried in vain to rise; he rested one hand on the cold floor and pointed around him with the other; illusions of dying filled his mind: "Look at the light there," he said quickly; "heavens! Elias! Elias! take me in your mantle of stars. Prophet! Elohi abi, my soul is thirsting for thee. Elias, there stands the cross of the disbelievers, dash it down! He comes, he comes, the messenger of the Lord! blessed be thy advent. Nissa, Nissa, there is your daughter, tear her away from the cross; the black monks want to dishonor the daughter of Israel! I am an old grey Jew, miserable fathers; Tisbet, the day of the Lord is not far off. Hosannah, hosannah! now they are gone the monks. Israel thy God is one, and only one."

Alonzo stepped forward; he raised the dying man from the earth and held him in his arms; his tears fell on the lifeless eye. The monks were silent.

"Give me back my grandchildern," stammered the old man, "bring them to me, Christian, that I may lay my hands upon them and bless them. What do you want here, Don Alonzo? here is the vault of deathc old and chilly as a prison."

"Your blessing, Arama," stammered Alonzo; "I am guiltless of your misfortunes."

The old man extended his hand, but it fell passively upon Alonzo's shoulder : "Esau, I have no blessing left for thee ; thou hast forfeited the birthright of the Lord."

His face now showed the convulsive struggle of death, but his eyes lit up once more, and reason returned at the last moment. The last words of his ascending spirit were,—"My King and Father, blessed be thy name in heaven and on earth ; be the glory of thy kingdom everlasting. Have mercy on me and bless my departure ; purify my soul and forgive me my sins. May thy justice reign over Israel, Amen." Arama was dead. Lay brothers carried the body and buried it in the near shrubbery. No monument marks his grave, but the old physician rests not the less tranquilly from his long pilgrimage.

As if nothing had happened, the Inquisitor now raised his eyes upon Alonzo, demanding of him a contrite confession of his sins ; he presented to him the necessity of clearing himself of the suspicion of secret Judaism, unless he wanted to draw upon himself the vengeance of the tribunal. Alonzo looked at him bitterly :

"Father Inquisitor, to be a Jew is bad, but surely it is worse to be a Christian. I know not the crime that brought me here. Is it my love for the pure maiden whom I worship, and who lost in this old man here her protector? I am then done with my confession and you know all."

Alonzo was questioned once more to ascertain to what degree Dinah had responded to his love ; and whether he had tried to make her adopt the Christian religion ; furthermore, about his relations to Abarbanel, and he was then remanded to prison in spite of his urgent appeals for liberty.

CHAPTER XXIII.

Who can describe the panic of the Jewish inhabitants of Spain, or the misery of the frightened families when they heard of the terrible decree? But the measure created no less consternation among the Christians. They were not so blind as not to perceive that these actions of the clergy would be the means of letting loose a wild and excited rabble, whose madness and fanaticism, once in full play, could not be stemmed. The Jew (as Abarbanel correctly stated) having no claims on the citizens, who might otherwise have been glad to rid themselves of hateful creditors, and by so doing free themselves of a social burden, but being on the contrary the means of support of both the nobles and people, to which latter class belonged for the most part those engaged in literary pursuits, the decree threatened the ruin of society. The people saw what political power the monks had gained over Spain, and that the bigotry of the rulers was the cause of those shameful deeds, and of the ruin of the country. The nobles especially were excited ; as in years past they were independent, but had latterly lost their property because they would not submit to the impositions of the monks ; and although they were not fond of the Jews, a similar fate united them in friendship, the more so as the latter had made themselves very serviceable to them by their intelligence, advice, and aid. Even among the Jews there were many who thought themselves powerful enough, in union with the new Christians, the Marannos, to resist by force° the edict, and win back their property even at the risk of their lives. Some were in hopes that the decree would be rescinded; others put their trust in heaven in expectation of a miracle; while others began to submit to necessity and sacrificed their goods. Many of the smaller communities not feeling secure there left for the larger cities. The monks and rulers could not fail to see the general excitement and felt no little fear at the desperation of the exiles. For this reason they ordered away the eminent Rabbis, to prevent them from still further exciting the people. For the same reason Torquemada issued the cruel order to the Christians, not to harbor, under pain of death, a Jewish exile, or give him even bread and water. In Granada also was the order read.

After Abarbanel's audience with the King, Jehuda had received from his father the order to remain in Granada, and use all his exertions to protect the southern communities. He entreated of him to put aside the frivolity of his youth, and by a steady firm behavior, become the leader and saviour of his people, saying, that he (Abarbanel) would remain in the north and in due time advice him what further to do. This advice was now hardly necessary for the youth. He had become a man. The last few months had robbed the world of its rosy illusions, and simple reality with its mountain pressure stood before him. His heart was wounded by hopeless love for the maiden he had hitherto looked upon only as a sister, but whose sympathy and liking for his imprisoned friend had now given definite shape to his feelings, that were till then vague and shadowy. His heart was mortified from wounded pride. He beheld the greatness of his father, which had seemed to him so unapproachable and advantageous, vanish. It was a terrible awakening from the morning dream of youth. In the first confusion of this awakening, when he should show himself an experienced and tried man, capable of extracting order from chaos, he found himself called upon to sacrifice himself for others at a time when he was most weak and stunned. And yet, perhaps, this very pressure of the outside world might become for him the healing balm, and all minor personal interests become merged and lost in the greater and nobler ones of the eternal world.

A change had also come over Dinah, which had a great effect on Jehuda. At first, when she had lost her paternal friend, and her lover, she passed into a state of mute grief. Nothing attracted her attention; she saw not the youth's struggle, nor the indescribable tenderness with which his eyes rested on her; nor his quiet tears, nor his fevered hands when touching hers, nor the shyness of his love as contrasted with its boldness as her brothers,—Alonzo and Arama were her only thoughts.

And when she now learned of the calamity impending over her whole nation, and when a letter written by a monk informed her of the fate of Arama, and when the suspicion of treachery was cast on Alonzo, she tore the image of her lover from her breast; and although she had doubts of his guilt, she was terrified at the deeds of the Inquisition towards her nation. To save them, to console them, to die for them, these were the only thoughts which in her magnanimity cast out all other thoughts, and filled her soul with new zeal for her faith. Then she sought the ancient writings ; the heroic deeds of Deborah

stood before her, the songs of David and the prophecies of
Isaiah animated her courage, and the more desperate the
crisis, the more urgent was the voice of her conscience. Jehuda
heard with amazement the words of the girl; and what the
teachings of the old man could not effect, was easily accom-
plished by her whom he loved; he became convinced of the
holiness of his faith, and felt himself capable of the highest
sacrifices.

CHAPTER XXIV.

The great Synagogue of Granada was thronged with the
devout; lamentations filled the air; old men sat weeping on
the floor of God, and their tears fell on the sacred volumes
containing the hymns of vanished liberty, from the mourning of
Jeremiah over the ruins of Jerusalem, down to the times when
the warriors of Europe again invaded Palestine, and commenced the deliverance of her people by slaughtering them.
The lamentations were followed by a solemn silence; after
which an old man began to sing the song of Jehuda Hallevy,
which he had often done when breathing out his soul under
the hoofs of a wild Arab steed. When the recitation was
finished, the scrolls of the law were taken from the Ark, and
they read the living word of God. Every one present listened
with undivided attention to the story of ancient days, when
Israel was driven away from the graves of their forefathers,
after the temple had been destroyed by fire, and Zion's citadel
had been wasted. Fifteen centuries had rolled away down
the stream of time, and yet the feet of the exiles found no
resting place in the land of their enemies and their captivity
did not cease.

Suddenly a maiden whose beauty surprised all, made her
way into the assembly. It was Dinah, the daughter of Nissa.
She kissed the scrolls of the law in the hands of the aged
Rabbi, and having ascended the steps leading to the holy ark,
spoke as follows:

"Men of Israel, you are amazed at the boldness of a maiden
in venturing to step upon this holy spot; but do not accuse

me of profanity towards the sanctuary on the very day when we lament that we must quit it. On such a day even the maiden takes courage to speak before her people, and the words of the prophet are fulfilled; 'Thy youths shall be prophets, and thy daughters shall foretell the future.' For the last time we are within these walls; already if the holy ark emptied of that treasure which we have preserved from Sinai. O, may it live in our hearts, and become a light to guide us through the dark path we have to tread ; may it be a hope to the wretched and a joy to our life ! The tempest of the Most High threatens us ; we are banished from our fatherland and know not whither to direct our steps. The priest is leveled with his people, the master with his servant, the rich with the poor. We have experienced many disasters through a long series of years ; but the Lord has ever spoken, 'Retire within thy chambers my people and shut the doors behind thee; hide thyself for a moment till my wrath shall have passed.' This time it is different ; the misery which has befallen us concerns not merely one person, family or community ; it falls upon all our brethren together. But what says the Lord of Hosts, most sacred in Israel. 'Stand still, that ye may see the salvation of the Lord.' By trusting and enduring, you will be strong. Let us now fulfill the command to trust in him and help will be surely nigh. Your ears will surely hear the words which a messenger of the Lord will whisper to you, 'This is the way in which ye shall go; stray not from it, neither go to the right hand nor the left.' But this way is the way of humiliation before the Lord, who will lead us over the mighty waters as he hath guided us through the wilderness. Let the people rage and the kings of the earth set themselves against us; we will quietly depart and no blood shall stain our temple. Let them take our houses ; we will camp under the eternal tent of heaven, till the Lord sends us intelligence whither we are to go, and where our brethren are assembled. No resistance, my brethren, to those spoilers ; for it would be a crime against the Lord, who shall send his judgment against the land that shall be waste and desolate. All her princes shall be as nothing, and thorns shall come up in her palaces, and nettles and thistles in her fortresses. But he will

strengthen our feeble hands.   The wilderness and the solitary
place shall be glad, and the desert shall rejoice and blossom
as a rose."

A melancholy joy filled the community, for they deemed
that Israel was not lost when maidens like this yet lived.   The
sacred scrolls were now carried away from the halls of the
synagogue, and the people followed with tears and lamentations.   Youths with drawn swords walked on both sides of the
scrolls ; but even the common class of people withdrew with
a holy reverence for it, in spite of their hatred for the Jews ;
they could not but acknowledge that out of Zion went forth
the law and the word of the Lord from Jerusalem.

CHAPTER XXV.

On the morning of the 5th of May, 1492, the bells were
ringing from the Cathedral of Granada, as the servants of the
Inquisition filled the streets and joined with the populace
crying, " Death to the Marannos." Louder and louder grew
the tumult in the open spaces and before the gates, while the
Jews in their houses trembled with fear, and commended their
souls to their Creator.   The timid concealed their jewels in
their clothes, while the braver shut the doors of their houses
and armed themselves.   The fury of the populace was now
excited to the highest pitch, and they attacked several houses,
maddened with the desire of murder and plunder.   They
spared neither the babe on the mother's breast, nor the wife
in the arms of husband, nor the sick and aged in their beds.
The floors of the rooms were reddened with blood as the
ruffian band spread slaughter far and wide, delighted at the
sight of the convulsions of the dying and the sound of their
victims' shrieks. All at once the voice of a herald was heard in
the streets, announcing to the poeple the king's order that
none of the Jews' property was to be touched as it was forfeited
to the State, and that the Jews themselves were to be removed
and conducted to the open space before the Alhambra.   The
servants of the Inquisition were withdrawn, the houses
occupied by soldiers and the inhabitants removed.

When this had been done the Rabbis addressed the authorities, and asked as their only request, that they be should permitted to visit ouec more the burial place before Granada. This was granted ; for it was easy in that place to defend them from the fury of the people.

In this dreadful hour, Jehuda and Dinah determined on dying together. They were in the house of Arama, and Dinah's tears flowed fast as she thought of her little charges, when the prior of the convent entered, accompanied by Gonzago and a crowd of followers who could scarcely be restrained from attacking the inmates in the room. The prior produced a decree of the Inquisition, commanding the maiden to be placed under the protection of the monastery together with the childern, who, as Arama, they stated, declared, were anxious to embrace Christianity. Jehuda threw himself between the maiden and the priests with his drawn sword, exclaiming that they should not touch her unless they first slew him.

But Dinah took his hand and whispered, "Retire Don Jehuda, and I will follow the men ; but you will first allow me, worthy prior, to take with me a precious jewel which I cannot leave here." With these words she hastened into an adjoining room, leaving the monks waiting impatiently. A cry was suddenly heard, "Save your lives, the house is in flames !" and smoke burst forth from all parts of the edifice.

With a cry of horror, Jehuda rushed into the chamber where Dinah had disappeared ; but the furious multitude swept him away with the children. Beam after beam fell with a loud crash, and the crackling flames rose up to the roof. Suddenly the maiden appeared there. Her looks wandered as she commended her soul to God, and she was on the point of falling into the flames, when a hideous looking man was seen to ascend to the roof and seize her, covering her with a ragged red clock. He then vanished as quickly as he appeared, by a tremendous leap into the adjoining gardens. They were seen no more, and the house was soon a heap of ashes, the mighty tomb of those who lay buried beneath the ruins.

CHAPTER XXVI.

The Jewish burial ground before the gates of Granada was built in the form of an amphitheatre. Here was many monuments to the memory of the dead. The white tombstones were covered with myrtles, and the whole scene was so quiet that it invited, as it were, the sleepers to rest in peace. In one corner stood a hall of white sandstone, bearing the incription, "He is the rock whose work is perfect, for all His ways are judgment; he is a God of truth and without iniquity, just and right is He." To this hall the multitude thronged, while some dispersed themselves among the tombs, where their tears mingled with the dewdrops that glittered on the blossoms of the wild thyme. An old man then ascended the steps of the hall, and with a faltering voice began to sing the words of the sacred Abodah in celebration of the Most High. The people sank on their knees and were absorbed in prayer, when clouds gathered on the horizon, and the heavens were darkened with their shadows. The sunlight grew dim and in the distance rolled thunder coming nearer and nearer. The sea rolled its waves more and more as the tempest agitated them; the lightning flashed and the elements struggled together with terrific force. Fear was depicted on every countenance, but the old man stood unmoved as the lightning played around him.

"The Lord has answered us," said he, "Listen my brethren, to the mighty voice that breaks from His sanctuary at sound of our prayers." And the people answered, "Amen."

But the tempest now grew more terrible, the earth trembled and shook to its foundations. The mountains of the Alpuxares burst asunder, and streams of fire gushed forth and rose up in flames to the sky, spreading a fearful light around the scene. The earth opened and whole villages were swallowed in the chasms which closed over them again and shut them in everlasting darkness.

Even Granada itself was troubled, for the ground on which it stood shook, the tops of the cathedrals were dashed to pieces, and whole palaces fell in ruins upon the inhabitants beneath.

Thus was the judgment of the Almighty shown against the Spaniards, and thus their fury against the Jews was silenced. They fled from their houses, which could not protect them, to the place where the Jewish community were praying. They clung to the cold tombstones, and listened to the voices of their victims.

"God has answered us," said the old man ; "the mountains tremble, but His mercy endureth forever. Let us now, my brethren, take our steps through the trembling earth, and turn ourselves to the sea; for the fury of our adversaries will awake with the day, and we shall again be persecuted. So farewell, Granada, and farewell, Spain ; we part forever."

Thus the community left Granada to join their brethren on the sea-shore; and, although the terrors of nature were rife around them, they trembled not, for when a man has lost his country, what can nature do to make him tremble whose hopes are passed and vanished ?

CHAPTER XXVII.

On the mountains of Gador, where the elements raged in all their fury, and the thunders rolled, and the torrents poured through their chasms in majestic cataracts, where the lofty beech trees were torn from their roots and thrown about in wild confusion, where the sound of a human voice had never been heard—there wandered the daughter of Nissa. Eight days and as many nights had she wandered, from rock to rock, and from desert to desert; roots were her only nourishment, and caves her resting place during the night. Every animal startled her with its footsteps, as she fancied she heard the feet of her enemies. Youthful and hopeful as she was, she at last began to despair when the terrors of nature were let loose upon her; and when she reflected that she was abandoned and alone, she sank down amid the thorny bushes, and a fainting fit made her unconscious of her misery. The rain fell from the heavens in floods, the lightning split the oak trees, and the earth quaked, but Dinah awoke not. And yet she was not quite alone. At her side stood a human being, an old man in rags. From his torn clothing, his grey locks, and his long beard, the rain dripped; his bare feet and arms were bleeding with the wounds from the brambles, but his eyes were fixed upon the maiden with tenderness and affection. From time to time he drew a dagger from under his garments, or broke out in a wild cry, as he stretched out his arms toward Dinah and screamed " Edla! Edla!" It was the o'd maniac, Morisco. It was he who had ascended the blazing roof and saved the maiden ; it was he who now wandered about with her in the wilderness and became the miserable companion of her sufferings. He now sat down beside her, and, tearing off his cloak, covered her with it, and wound some flowers into a wreath and laid it on her dripping ringlets.

Suddenly the sound of trumpets was heard, and Dinah awoke.

"They are the trumpets of my people," she exclaimed ; " they are the notes of lamentation, which speak of wretchedness and the sorrows of Israel's history."

She seized the hand of the old man, who willingly followed her, and ascended an eminence to view the sight. But who could describe the prospect which opened before them? The tempest had ceased, and the sun shone forth over the broad mirror of the deep. On the sea, which was stretched before them were some ships, and on the shore was the camp of Israel. Oh, Jacob! thy tents are not so goodly, nor thy tabernacles so fair, as when Beor's son blessed thee; and yet thy sight is refreshing to the banished, for yonder is safety.

The trumpets blew louder and louder, calling to the last worship in the land of Iberia. All the Jewish communities were encamped there, for the King had promised them ships to convey them ; but the few which he sent could not convey the third part of them, and those who were left were menaced with slavery if they did not deny their God.

Thither the steps of the Jewish maiden and the Moorish maniac hastened, and he whom they first met was Alonzo, the Spanish captain. After Arama's death and the fruitless efforts of the monks to possess themselves of the maiden, he had been set at liberty. He found Arama's house reduced to ashes, and he heard of the miraculous disappearance of the maiden, but he could not reconcile himself to her being dead. He therefore betook himself to the Jewish encampment, and now he saw her again. But the bloom of her beauty was destroyed; her limbs trembled with fever, and, casting on him a look in which resignation and love were depicted, she fell fainting on the ground, and was carried away into a tent hard by. Weeks passed on, and more than once Dinah lay on the threshold of the grave; but Alonzo never left her, although he scarcely wished her to live, when her life would be but a scene of sorrow, without happiness and without love.

CHAPTER XXVIII.

" Hark! the voice of a multitude on the mountains like as a great people—a tumultuous noise as of the kingdoms of nations gathered together. The stars of heaven and the con-stellations thereof do not give their light; the sun is darkened in his going forth, and the moon does not cause her light to shine. The Lord shakes the heavens, and the earth removes out of her place. They are like the chased roe, and as a sheep that no man taketh up. Every one that is found is thrust through, and every one that is joined unto them falls by the sword. Their children also are dashed to pieces before their eyes, their houses spoiled, and their wives ravished. And it is as with the people, so with the priest; as with the servant, so with his master; as with the maid, so with her mistress; as with the lender, so with the borrower."

Thus sang the divine prophet Isaiah in ancient times, and thus the communities of Spain, from the East and from the West, were encamping in the mountains of Cuenca. Don Isaac Abarbanel was at their head. He, a king among captives, led the Marannos on their rapid road. He tendered assistance to the widows and orphans; through his care the suffering were protected and the old relieved; he upheld those that were laid low; he consoled those that mourned; he suffered and prayed with his people. At last the offspring of Israel's kings has regained his greatness, and has taken to himself the inheritance of Judah and Israel. In the palaces of Madrid and Seville he was a slave, but now he is a king. He has sacrificed his property to his nation, and will leave nothing to his sons but his chains.

Thus they wandered on in the name of the Lord. The gates of the towns were shut against them, and, by an order of Ximenes, no house would give them shelter or furnish them with bread, so that they encamped under the tents of heaven, and kissed the fatherland which exiled them. Not, as before, was the Ark of the Covenant borne before them by the priests of the Lord; but the angel yet lives who guided them through the wilderness, and as yet they have kept in safety the jewel of the law.

Carthago Nova opens its ports, and Italy, Parthenope, Rome, are the destinations of their voyages, for there the priests are not fanatics, and there the spirit of love still reigns.

Farewell to Spain, where their fathers slept, where the myrtle ever flourished for the festival day, and where the priests of their people taught.

A west wind arose as they set sail, and the sun went down in a scarlet glow; but Abarbanel lay with his face on the deck, and muttered the words of the Prophet: "Lift up thy voice, my people; shout ye, rejoice ye at the name of the Lord. Worship the Lord in caves, and upon the isles of the sea worship the name of the Lord."

CHAPTER XXIX.

The tent into which Dinah had been carried belonged to a blind widow woman, and by her kind attentions and the natural vigor of youth, Dinah soon conquered the attempts of death, and the rose of health again began to bloom upon her cheeks. But the presence of her beloved still filled her with a melancholy feeling, for she had determined to quit, if she could not forget him. And oh! if the inward struggle of the heart be painful in the days of happiness, what must it be when it comes amid the roughness and misery of misfortune?

Like a guardian genius, Alonzo was ever near her, guarding the tent in which she dwelt with the blind widow and the old maniac Moor, who could not be persuaded to leave her. He did not hesitate even to stand among the ranks of abandoned Israel, and to eat with them bread moistened with tears, and to endure the mockery of their oppressors.

"Dinah," said he, one morning, "the communities of Israel in Barbary have sent ships for us ; do you feel strong enough to enter upon our voyage thither ?"

"I feel strong enough for the voyage, Don Alonzo ; but only without you shall I leave Spain. Here we must part for ever."

She spoke these words in a voice which betrayed the inward struggle, and when she had finished she burst into a flood of tears. Alonzo stood silently.

"Noble youth," continued she, "it is time that we should make our resolution. Yes, I love you with all the ardor of first love of which a maiden is capable. But my lot is resignation. I shall join in the misery of my people, while your destiny is a higher one. Serve your Spain with all the vigor of youth ; or go to France, or Germany, and seek laurels for your brow. Do not give up your fortune for so low a prize as a poor Jewess. I cannot, I shall never be yours. By the name of my father," said she, while her eyes were raised to heaven like those of some blessed angel, "I shall never be yours."

"Oh, Dinah !" said Alonzo, "you have broken my heart."

"Not so, Don Alonzo ; look at the feeble maiden ; she has conquered. And believe me it is better so. Where is Jehuda Abarbanel ? He risked all to save me, and now he languishes, perhaps, in prison. Where are Arama's children? You must find them out and save them. Oh, if I had not to risk more than life I would not stand here."

Alonzo felt her reproach ; and the old man, who stood at her side and saw her weep, said in an affecting voice : "Oh, she weeps—my Edla ! Do not let her weep, young man, do not let her weep, and I will love you as Allah loves Edla."

At this moment a noise was heard before the tent, and Gonzago Campanton entered, accompanied by some soldiers and other persons. Dinah uttered a loud shriek ; but before

the monk could utter a word, the old Moor rushed forward
and plunged his dagger in his breast, exclaiming: "Black,
diabolical monster, the Morisco knows how to strike!"

A cry of horror re-echoed through the tent. The monk's
eyes rolled wildly, and at last fell on the blind Jewess, who
sat in a corner. He rushed to her, crying out: "Mother!
mother, yuor Gonzago is dying at your side ; cursed be the
day of my birth, cursed to be the day of my death." The blind
woman staggered; and, rushing forward, she fell upon the
monk, while his streaming blood ran over her blind eyes,
as she heard the death-rattle in his throat. He lay on the
ground, beating his wounded breast with his hands; and
while his eyes rolled strangely aroud the place, he uttered
some Hebrew words of repentance and expired. The soldiers
meanwhile had surrounded the old Moor, who stood quietly
brandishing his dagger; and, as they led him away, his shouts
of joy were heard in the distance : "Thus saith the Lord God
of Hosts: 'Consider ye, and call for the mourning women,
that they may come. And let them make haste, and take up
a wailing for us, that our eyes may run down with tears,
and our eyelids may gush out with waters. For a voice of
wailing is heard out of Zion.'"

*   *   *   *   *   *   *   *   *   *   *   *

The captain hastened, and the anchors were weighed.
Alonzo seized Dinah's hand and led her to the shore. Long
did they stand in that last embrace, and the waves of the
ocean could not be more agitated than their hearts.

"Farewell, Dinah! We shall meet again in heaven."

"Farewell, farewell, Alonzo!"

And, as they said these words, a light breeze sprang up
and filled the sails, and the ship glided through the blue
waters. But Alonzo turned aside in silence to weep.

CHAPTER XXX.

On the banks of the Guadalquiver, at the foot of Mount
Alcarez, stands a castle with four towers, built by the ancient

Goths. In one of these towers Jehuda Abarbanel was confined. From the window at which he stood he cast a searching look over the river, but not a human creature was visible. The place seemed to be the picture of death. A few soldiers, with some prisoners and lay-brethren of the Inquisition, seemed to be the only inhabitants of the castle; and on the opposite side of the river rose numbers of rocks, in which eagles had built their nests. Every day a lay-brother brought Jehuda his scanty meal; but all his attempts to elicit from him some words were fruitless, although his looks indicated that he was not quite indifferent to the fate of the prisoner, as he often fixed a tearful eye upon him, and complied with his desire in bringing him a mandolin.

On the evening of which we were speaking, Jehuda was looking through his barred window at the moon, which shed her full lustre upon the waters of the river, as they splashed against the high walls of the castle. Melancholy took possession of his heart, and he took the mandolin and sang to its accompaniment a song, which may be thus rendered:

'Tis but vain! the lyre is sad
'Neath the trembling finger,
And the notes of mirthful songs
Hushed in silence linger.
Oh, my lyre! thy joyous string
Will not bear the waking,
For 'tis all in vain to sing
When the heart is breaking.

Wherefore should I strive to smile
By a false endeavor?
Wherefore join the mirth whose sound
Soon shall cease for ever?
For the blight of grief hath past
On this youthful bosom,
And beneath the cutting blast
Chilled is every blossom.

Oh. then let my mandolin
Tempt no songs of pleasure,
But with sad and solemn notes
Thrill in lowly measure.
Though my heart from joys around,
Nought of hope may borrow,
Yet will Music's mournful sound
Teach me how to sorrow.

Suddenly he perceived a boat floating on the waves; and in it he saw two men, bending the course of the vessel toward his cell. At this moment the lay-brother entered.

"Your deliverance is near," whispered he; "hasten and follow me, in the name of the God of Israel."

Jehuda followed the man, and without being perceived by any one they descended the narrow staircase which led to a small gate at which the boat was landed. The lay-brother was the first to jump into it; Jehuda followed him, and they all rowed down the stream in silence and with the greatest rapidity.

When the morning dawned, they stopped before a rock. "Now we may speak," said the lay-brother to Jehuda; "you are among your own brethren; follow me to the cave of the Marannos."

The boat was hidden among the reeds on the shore, and the four men entered a cave, the entrance of which was over-grown with thorns and brambles, and the walls covered with moss. The cave became wider and wider, and led them to an extensive space, where Jehuda was surprised to find an assembly of several hundred persons of all ranks—monks, soldiers and citizens—but all wearing white scarfs around their heads, while their countenances expressed suffering and pain. The space was lighted with wax lights. Upon a large stone, covered with a white cloth, lay the scroll of the law of Moses, and in the corners of the cave were curtains belonging to the holy ark, gold and silver vases, and numberless books. On entering the assembly, Jehuda cried, "Lo ammi!" This was the watch-word of the Marannos in Spain, who had assumed the exterior form of Christianity but in their hearts preserved their ancient faith, and, in the obscurity of night, held their meetings in caves and ruined edifices, to keep up some connection among themselves.

They had just finished the morning service, and the elders, approaching Jehuda, thus addressed him: "You are among your brethren, whom we have saved from prison and certain death. You are the only one of your family on the Spanish soil, for your father has reached Italy. We need the vigor of youth to confirm us in our belief, and we entreat you to remain in Spain and not to abandon your brethren. But before you decide, remain with us this one day, for we celebrate to-day the siege of the Temple."

A solemn silence pervaded the assembly, until some of them stepped forward and gave accounts of the fate of their brethren in the different towns. Collections were then made for the suffering, the distressed, and the poor. Among those who appeared most active was a Franciscan monk, who had become a member of the Inquisition in order that he might use his influence in saving his co-religionists; for it was a common custom among the Marannos to enter some monkish order, because, in their solitary cells they had the best opportunity for performing the rites of their ancient religion.

They then collected together again, and uttered prayers and lamentations which might have moved the very walls. Jehuda's soul was powerfully agitated ; and although he felt sorry for this secresy and concealment, he still sympathized deeply with his brethren in misfortune. He, therefore, became one of them under the assumed name of Leon. When night came on, they were all dismissed through a different opening of the cave, which led into a valley, to various parts of which they dispersed, to re-unite again at the appointed day of the new moon.

CHAPTER XXXI.

On the 21th of February, 1495, the army of Charles VIII. of France made its triumphant entry into Naples—for the French monarch had been at war with King Alphonso of Naples, and had expelled him from his capital. The King of France entered with all the pomp of a Greek emperor, for the troops of Arragon had been defeated before the town, and the cowardly Neapolitans humbly delivered the keys into the hands of the foreign king. Immense crowds filled the streets, and the French entered the houses to plunder them, although contrary to the orders of their commanders. The Ghetto was, above all, exposed to their fury ; and the intoxicated soldiers went there and returned laden with the spoils of the Jews.

Before one house of the Ghetto, which was distinguished above all the rest by its cleanly appearance, a number of these rapacious soldiery were assembled. Joined by the people, they had forced the gates, and were entering the house when they were met by a man of noble appearance, whose unusual dignity of gesture, high, open forehead and penetrating eye commanded respect. Beside him stood a maiden of pale but beautiful features. The man was Don Isaac Abarbanel, and the maiden, Dinah, his foster-daughter.

"Do you want my house and my treasures?" said he to the soldiers; "here they are."

Having said these words, he took Dinah by the hand and led her into the street. The multitude were at first amazed, but their avarice soon revived, and they entered the house, raising loud cries of joy.

When Dinah had landed from the ship in Italy, Abarbanel had received her into his house at Naples, where the magnanimity of King Ferdinand had opened an asylum for the fugitive Marannos. Thousands from the banks of the Tejo and the Guadalquiver found a resting-place at the foot of Vesuvius. This wonderful man, Abarbanel, had risen into notice even at the court of the king of Naples; and, as in former times, he employed his influence to aid his suffering co-religionists. But, although he advanced in years, he received no intelligence of his beloved son. Yet Dinah was to him some consolation. She cheered his solitary hours, reminded him of the several incidents of his eventful life, and dwelt upon the circumstances that testified his noble endeavors. But her own heart was broken; for when once love has arisen in woman's breast, it is a tender and beautiful flower, and woe when the tempest touches it, for henceforth it will but bring forth branches and leaves, but no blossom to adorn them.

As they stepped out of the Ghetto, the train of the king passed, attended by all the nobles and knights. But amid them was one distinguished by his noble and handsome features, who cast his eyes around the crowd. At last they fell on the Jewish maiden, and their eyes met. His face flushed scarlet, while she grew pale, and leant for support upon her companion. The train passed on; but still the knight looked backward upon Dinah, who, at length, recovered herself, and begged Abarbanel to accelerate their steps. They did so, and reached at length a hut on the sea-shore at Portici, where they took shelter for the night.

No sleep visited the eyes of Dinah on that night; restless and uneasy, she passed it in dreams and meditations, and when the morning sun arose, gilding the smoke of Vesuvius, and when the voices of the morning birds were heard from the lemon-trees, she knelt down before the hut and breathed a prayer to Jehovah, the God of love. Engaged in devotion, she did not perceive that the knight who yesterday had seen her was now standing by her side. He was a brave general of King Charles, who had taken Capua, and defeated the armies of Arragon—he was Don Fernando Alonzo. She looked up, and he stood before her.

"Do you know me, Dinah?" said he.

At this moment Abarbanel stepped out of the hut, and she rushed to Abarbanel and embraced him.

"Don Alonzo," said she, sobbing, "here must our journeys part; you must pursue glory along the paths of fortune, and leave grief and love to the Maranno."

"Nay, Dinah," said he, "I have been ever true to thee; in the storm of the battle, in the hour of danger, in the day of glory. But one more look, but one more pressure of the hand, and I will depart."

She held out her hand to him covered with tears, like dew-drops on a lily, and hid her face on Abarbanel's breast, while the knight hastened away.

The same evening his house and property were restored to Abarbanel, and guards were sent to protect him from injury. He did not, however choose to stay, but followed his exiled king to Sicily, whither Dinah accompanied him.

CHAPTER XXXII.

Corfu is an island in the Ionian sea. The spring had commenced here; the birds had begun to rouse themselves to melody, and the snow on the mountains had begun to melt before the rays of the warm sunlight. The banks of the brooks were covered with flowers, the trees put forth their blossoms, and near the waters of the silver stream the sweet lily reared her pearly bud. The woods resounded with the songs of birds; roses, honeysuckles, and acacias breathed their scents around. The bee left her cave in the hollow oak, where she had deposited her honey, and began once more to gather the juices of the flowers, and to flutter around the freshened trees. The inhabitants of the coast got their nets ready for new draughts, and put their boats and other apparatus in good order; while the industrious peasant led his flock to enjoy the rich herbage of the meadows, where all the beautiful plants and flowers of Greece lent their delights to the scene.

Not far from the coast were several houses inhabited by families of Spanish emigrants, who were much beloved by the quite inhabitants for their kindness and unobtrusive behaviour. They had been instructed by the peasants in the methods of agriculture, and were hence enabled to produce good and sufficient crops. But among the first of these persons was Don Isaac Abarbanel, who, among his brethren in exile, was considered the wisest, the noblest, and the best. Well experienced in the holy law, and of the seed of David of the house of Bethlehem, he had been banished from Portugal to Spain, from Spain to Naples, whence he was compelled to go to Messina, and at last he had sought a refuge among the isles of Greece. But the hairs of his forehead had grown grey ; his high figure began to sink under the Psalmist of Israel, "They afflicted me from my youth, yet they have not prevailed against me. The ploughers have ploughed upon my back ; they made long their furrows." And by his side was his true partner in all his trouble and exile, Dinah. For the third time had she done her duty as a child, and fulfilled the commandment of the law. The storm of passion had left her modest bosom, and was totally subdued. From the dawn of the day, when the sun shed his first rays from the shores of Ionia into the cheerful apartment, until the shadows of the evening fell upon the ocean, she lived only for the exiled sage. Abarbanel often listened to her with devotion as she poured out the feelings of recollection in soft strains on the turf under the lytiscus trees. Often during the day, when he was exhausted by reflections on his own fate, and by studious researches into the word of God, it was the voice of Dinah that refreshed his heart ; and when the prophecies of the divine prophet of Israel, Isaiah the son of Amoz, had inspired his spirit, it was the Castilian song which led him back to the land of his youth, or the lamentation of the ancient poets over the fall of Zion which drew tears from his aged eyes. Thus the exiled Maranno could look both to the East and to the West, though far from both, and could gaze on one side at the ruins of the Temple in Palestine, and on the other, at the wreck of his domestic happiness in the valleys of Iberia ; but often would he sigh, and his spirit would murmur forth, "O, that I had wings like a dove, for then would I fly away and be at rest."

It was the day of Sabbath ; a holy repose was observed in the house, and repose was in his heart. He lay slumbering on the divan, and at his side sat Dinah in a festival dress, his head leaning on her arm.

A gentle knock was heard at the door, and a man of middle age, in a pilgrim's dress, entered the room. He looked around, and, seeing Dinah, burst into tears, and covered his head with his hands.

Abarbanel awoke at the sound, and raising himself up, said, "Who are you, and what do you want here?"

The stranger raised his head, and rushing forward, fell upon Abarbanel's neck, crying, "It is I, your son; do you know your son, my father?"

The father streched out his arms and clasped him to his heart, shedding tears of joy, while Dinah fell on her knees in thankfulness.

"Blessed be the Lord who loosens those that are bound, and lifteth up those that are bent down ! To Him be greatness, and power, and glory, and majesty, for ever and ever !"

Our tale is almost done ; a few closing words are necessary to satisfy the natural interest of the Reader as to the facts of its principal characters.

The old maniac Moor contrived by some means to escape from his guards, and to take refuge in the mountains; and he was never afterwards seen.

Alonzo, upon parting with Dinah, felt that the object of his life was gone, and that, whatever he might do, he should never find any earthly happiness. The hope of an early death was his only consolation, and he sought it upon the battle field. On the bank of the Taro, a sanguinary conflict took place between the troops of Charles and Ferdinand, and Alonzo, leading the soldiers under the banner of Charles to victory, found the consolation he sought, in death.

Arama's children, who were baptized and brought up in the Christian faith, when they attained their age of reason and understanding, emigrated to a far off land and returned to the faith of their fathers.

But Jehuda and Dinah—what of them? Suffice to say that, as they lived together, their hearts grew dearer to one another day by day, cut off as they were from all hopes and pleasures from without. Under the influence of no blind and tempestuous passion, but touched by deep and undivided affection, they were wedded according to the especial desire of Abarbanel, whose years, though spent in sorrow, closed in 'happiness after seeing the union of his beloved children. And although Dina's first admirer lay cold and silent on the battle-field of the Taro, she did not forget him, and often would Dinah and Jehuda feelingly talk together of the noble character and the disinterested love of the Christian Captain, Alonzo.

www.ingramcontent.com/pod-product-compliance
Lightning Source LLC
Chambersburg PA
CBHW020028030726
47499CB00007B/2325